Cara took a deep, shaky breath. She looked straight ahead at the line of the hills rather than at Steven. "The real reason we went to London was because Mom was being considered for a big promotion."

"Well, that's great. Isn't it?"

"You don't understand," she told him. "A promotion—and a transfer."

"A transfer?"

"They called her on Monday, after we got back to Sweet Valley. She got the job in the London office. She starts in three weeks." Cara's voice dropped to a whisper. "Steven, my mother and I—we're moving to London."

Slowly, Cara turned to face Steven. He stared back at her, but he couldn't speak or move his hands to touch her. It was as if the shock had drained all the power from his body, all the blood from his heart.

Finally, he managed to stutter, "You can't. You can't go."

"Do you think I want to?" Cara cried.

Steven reached for Cara. He held her as tightly as he could, but even so he felt as if she were already slipping through his fingers.

Bantam Books in the Sweet Valley High series
Ask your bookseller for the books you have missed

#1 DOUBLE LOVE
#2 SECRETS
#3 PLAYING WITH FIRE
#4 POWER PLAY
#5 ALL NIGHT LONG
#6 DANGEROUS LOVE
#7 DEAR SISTER
#8 HEARTBREAKER
#9 RACING HEARTS
#10 WRONG KIND OF GIRL
#11 TOO GOOD TO BE TRUE
#12 WHEN LOVE DIES
#13 KIDNAPPED!
#14 DECEPTIONS
#15 PROMISES
#16 RAGS TO RICHES
#17 LOVE LETTERS
#18 HEAD OVER HEELS
#19 SHOWDOWN
#20 CRASH LANDING!
#21 RUNAWAY
#22 TOO MUCH IN LOVE
#23 SAY GOODBYE
#24 MEMORIES
#25 NOWHERE TO RUN
#26 HOSTAGE!
#27 LOVESTRUCK
#28 ALONE IN THE CROWD
#29 BITTER RIVALS
#30 JEALOUS LIES
#31 TAKING SIDES
#32 THE NEW JESSICA
#33 STARTING OVER
#34 FORBIDDEN LOVE
#35 OUT OF CONTROL
#36 LAST CHANCE
#37 RUMORS
#38 LEAVING HOME
#39 SECRET ADMIRER
#40 ON THE EDGE
#41 OUTCAST
#42 CAUGHT IN THE MIDDLE

#43 HARD CHOICES
#44 PRETENSES
#45 FAMILY SECRETS
#46 DECISIONS
#47 TROUBLEMAKER
#48 SLAM BOOK FEVER
#49 PLAYING FOR KEEPS
#50 OUT OF REACH
#51 AGAINST THE ODDS
#52 WHITE LIES
#53 SECOND CHANCE
#54 TWO-BOY WEEKEND
#55 PERFECT SHOT
#56 LOST AT SEA
#57 TEACHER CRUSH
#58 BROKENHEARTED
#59 IN LOVE AGAIN
#60 THAT FATAL NIGHT
#61 BOY TROUBLE
#62 WHO'S WHO?
#63 THE NEW ELIZABETH
#64 THE GHOST OF
    TRICIA MARTIN
#65 TROUBLE AT HOME
#66 WHO'S TO BLAME?
#67 THE PARENT PLOT
#68 THE LOVE BET
#69 FRIEND AGAINST FRIEND
#70 MS. QUARTERBACK
#71 STARRING JESSICA!
#72 ROCK STAR'S GIRL
#73 REGINA'S LEGACY
#74 THE PERFECT GIRL
#75 AMY'S TRUE LOVE
#76 MISS TEEN SWEET VALLEY
#77 CHEATING TO WIN
#78 THE DATING GAME
#79 THE LONG-LOST BROTHER
#80 THE GIRL THEY BOTH LOVED
#81 ROSA'S LIE
#82 KIDNAPPED BY THE CULT!
#83 STEVEN'S BRIDE

Super Editions: PERFECT SUMMER
SPECIAL CHRISTMAS
SPRING BREAK
MALIBU SUMMER
WINTER CARNIVAL
SPRING FEVER

Super Thrillers: DOUBLE JEOPARDY
ON THE RUN
NO PLACE TO HIDE
DEADLY SUMMER

Super Stars: LILA'S STORY
BRUCE'S STORY
ENID'S STORY
OLIVIA'S STORY

Magna Edition: THE WAKEFIELDS OF SWEET VALLEY

STEVEN'S
BRIDE

Written by
Kate William

Created by
FRANCINE PASCAL

BANTAM BOOKS

NEW YORK • TORONTO • LONDON • SYDNEY • AUCKLAND

RL 6, IL age 12 and up

STEVEN'S BRIDE

A Bantam Book / March 1992

Sweet Valley High is a registered trademark of Francine Pascal

Conceived by Francine Pascal

Produced by Daniel Weiss Associates, Inc.
33 West 17th Street
New York, NY 10011

Cover art by James Mathewuse

ISBN 0-553-29229-3

Published simultaneously in the United States and Canada

*Bantam Books are published by Bantam Books, a division of Bantam
Doubleday Dell Publishing Group, Inc. Its trademark, consisting of the
words "Bantam Books" and the portrayal of a rooster, is Registered
in U.S. Patent and Trademark Office and in other countries. Marca
Registrada. Bantam Books, 666 Fifth Avenue, New York, New York
10103.*

PRINTED IN THE UNITED STATES OF AMERICA

OPM   0 9 8 7 6 5 4 3 2 1

To Megan Walsh

One

"What's so funny?" Jessica Wakefield asked her friend Cara Walker, who had just burst out laughing. It was a typically perfect southern California Saturday, and the two girls, both juniors at Sweet Valley High, were reclining on lounge chairs by the pool in Jessica's backyard. They weren't alone. Earlier, Jessica's older brother, Steven, a college freshman and Cara's steady boyfriend, had announced his intention to fire up the grill for a cookout. To Jessica and her twin sister, Elizabeth, it had sounded like a good excuse for a party. They had gotten on the phone to some of their friends immediately.

"I was just thinking," Cara replied, "how if for some strange reason I were having a hard time telling you and Elizabeth apart, I'd only have to look at your reading material to figure out who was who."

1

Jessica glanced down at her glossy fashion magazine. Then she looked over at her sister. Sure enough, Elizabeth was halfway through a novel that looked as if it weighed as much as she did.

Jessica and Elizabeth had identical physical features—the same perfect size-six figure, sun-streaked blond hair, sparkling blue-green eyes, and a tiny dimple in the left cheek. But they were different in many ways, and Cara had just pointed out one of them. Elizabeth was known as the serious twin; she was a conscientious student and a columnist for the school newspaper. Because she aspired to be a professional writer, she read all sorts of things—poetry and short stories, fiction and nonfiction. Jessica, on the other hand, considered reading for fun a contradiction in terms. She would rather play tennis or go shopping or rent a movie. After all, she had a reputation to uphold. Sure, Elizabeth went to her share of parties, but no one at Sweet Valley High knew better how to have a good time than Jessica Wakefield.

Occasionally, though, Jessica resented the way people categorized her and Elizabeth. It seemed as if people assumed that Jessica and Elizabeth were complete opposites. And because Elizabeth was everything *good*, Jessica was seen as everything bad. If Elizabeth was smart and studious, Jessica was lazy; if Elizabeth was considerate, Jessica was selfish; if Elizabeth was reliable, Jessica was irresponsible. In fact, not very long before, Jessica had experienced an identity crisis. As a result of lying to her parents about her failing grade in math, she had been grounded. Suddenly Jessica had begun to feel as if everyone, including her family and her boyfriend, Sam Woodruff, had turned against her. Desperate to find someone who believed in her, she had become involved with a cult. Remembering how close she had come to losing touch with reality, Jessica shivered. She had learned the hard way that self-esteem had to come from the *inside*. She was one of the lucky ones. She had come to believe in herself again, and now she was glad for all the ways in which she was different from Elizabeth. It was what made her unique.

"What is that, Liz?" Jessica asked her twin. *"War and Peace?"*

"Close." Elizabeth smiled. *"Anna Karenina."*

"Nice light weekend reading," remarked Elizabeth's best friend, Enid Rollins.

"I can't put it down," Elizabeth confessed.

Jessica turned back to Cara. "Well, compared to Tolstoy, this magazine might *look* flimsy, but it's really very educational."

Amy Sutton snorted. "I'm sure you're learning tons. How *are* the movie stars wearing their hair these days?"

Jessica tapped a page of the magazine. "This article is about how to balance marriage and a career in the nineties."

"But Jessica, you're only sixteen," Steven reminded her as he hoisted himself out of the swimming pool and reached for a dry towel.

"True," Jessica admitted. "And I don't plan to get married for decades—"

"Phew," Sam said.

Jessica swatted him playfully with the magazine. "And I have no idea what kind of career I want. But that doesn't mean I can't get a head start on the balancing part."

Wrapping the towel around his waist, Steven crossed the patio to the grill to light the coals. Cara followed him, a bottle of sunscreen in her hand.

"Good idea," Jessica observed. "Really slather it on him, Cara. He's as pale as a mushroom!"

"When was the last time you were out in the sun?" Elizabeth's boyfriend, Todd Wilkins, asked Steven.

"It feels like months." Steven grinned wryly. "I hate to admit it, but I rarely go anywhere these days without an armload of books. I even study at the stoplights!"

"That's sick," Jessica remarked.

"I think it's wonderful," Elizabeth countered. "It'll all be worth it when you get into that pre-law program!"

Steven put a match to the coals and nodded. "I hope so."

Jessica watched her brother closely. He *had* been studying hard lately, probably harder than he ever had in his life, and to Jessica's eye, the

4

strain was starting to show. But Elizabeth was right. It *would* be worth it. For as long as Jessica could remember, Steven had wanted to be a lawyer like his father, a prominent Sweet Valley attorney. A few months earlier, he had applied to a special program at the university that would take him straight through law school. He would earn a combined B.A. and J.D. in six years instead of the usual seven. The program was very competitive and only a handful of students were accepted each year. Jessica sighed. Steven's getting accepted would be only the start. With extra coursework, case studies, and practical experience in a law office, the pressure would probably never let up! Still, Jessica knew her brother had his heart set on getting into the program. It would be the opportunity of a lifetime.

"Just don't overdo it," Sam advised. "Remember, all work and no play . . ."

"Well, hey, look at me now." Steven flourished the barbecue tongs. "Am I relaxed or what?"

"Definitely a man of leisure," Todd confirmed. "What brought you out of the library, anyway?"

Steven put an arm around Cara's shoulders. "I wanted to spend some time with Cara before she leaves for London tomorrow," he explained. Pulling Cara close, Steven kissed her cheek lightly. "I'll miss you," he whispered.

Cara pushed him away. "Don't make such a

big deal about it," she snapped. "I'll only be gone a week!"

Steven raised his eyebrows, surprised by her sudden grumpiness.

Jessica's eyes grew dreamy. "London. I'm so jealous!"

Cara shrugged. "From everything I've heard, it's just another big, dirty city."

"Will you take any day trips, like to Stratford-on-Avon?" asked Elizabeth. "I know *I'd* love to visit Shakespeare's birthplace."

"Probably not," Cara said. "It's just a stupid business trip. My mom will be tied up in meetings all day."

"Oh, come on, Cara," Amy protested. "I bet you'll have a blast. You can sightsee on your own while your mother's at her meetings. And if nothing else, you'll be missing a week of school!"

"Well, *I've* been to London, numerous times," Lila Fowler drawled. The daughter of a wealthy computer-chip manufacturer, Lila never let pass an occasion to remind her friends that she had traveled extensively in Europe. "It's not Paris, but the shopping is still pretty good."

"Yeah, and those big black taxis and red double-decker buses," contributed Enid. "Very romantic!"

Jessica sighed enviously. "I would love to be in your place, Cara!"

*   *   *

6

Steven studied Cara's tense profile, his own expression thoughtful and concerned. "I'm going inside to get the burgers," he announced. He touched Cara's arm. "Want to help me out?"

Cara trailed after him through the sliding glass door into the Spanish-tiled kitchen. As soon as they were out of sight of the others, Steven wrapped her in a tight hug.

Cara laughed in spite of herself. "Did we come in here for food or romance?"

"A little of both," Steven said with a grin. "It's a good combination, I think."

He bent his head to kiss her. For a moment she responded, then she moved her mouth away from his. Steven frowned. He and Cara had been dating for a while; they were very much in love, and very close. Steven had come to know Cara almost as well as he knew himself, and right now he was certain she had something troublesome on her mind. It wasn't like her to be moody; she was usually so caring and open.

Steven brushed a strand of glossy dark hair back from Cara's olive-skinned cheek. "Cara, what's wrong? Is something bothering you?"

"Of course not." Cara stepped away, turning her back to him. "What would be bothering me?"

"Well, I don't know, that's why I'm asking," Steven replied. "Is it something to do with the trip to London? Your mom's not having problems at work, is she?"

"No way." Cara laughed, somewhat bitterly,

Steven thought. "Exactly the opposite. Since she and Dad got divorced, she's become a total career woman."

"Good for her," Steven commented.

"Yeah, good for her." Steven saw Cara take a deep breath. When she faced him again, she was smiling, but it looked like the kind of smile that required a conscious effort—it didn't quite reach her brown-velvet eyes. "Nothing's wrong," Cara assured him. "Sorry if I'm cranky. I guess—I guess it's just that I'll miss you."

She slipped her arms around Steven's waist and pressed her face against his chest. Steven kissed her hair. He wasn't entirely convinced, but he didn't push it. He and Cara were going steady, but that didn't mean they had to share every single thought with each other. She would confide in him if and when she was ready. "It's like you said, though," Steven told her. "It's just a week, right?"

Cara nodded, but she didn't lift her head to meet Steven's eyes. "Just a week," she confirmed.

Steven chuckled. "You haven't even left yet, and already I can't wait until you get back."

Cara squeezed him tightly. "Me, either," she whispered.

"I'll be there in an hour," Cara announced on the other end of the phone.

Steven glanced at the clock radio on his desk. It was Thursday evening, and he had just

8

returned from dinner at the cafeteria. He had hoped to get in five or six hours of studying before he went to bed. "I'm kind of swamped with work," he told Cara. "I really can't—"

"I won't bother you," Cara promised. "I'll let you read. I can't stay too long, anyway. It *is* a school night."

"So maybe you shouldn't come up," Steven pointed out. "Look, tomorrow's Friday. I'm driving down to Sweet Valley after my intramural soccer game. I'll see you then."

"But I need to see you tonight," Cara insisted. Steven couldn't ignore the intensity in Cara's voice. "I just *have* to see you. OK?"

Steven sighed. "Well . . . yeah, OK. Look, I want to see you, too. But I'm not kidding about being swamped. I have my political science seminar tomorrow."

"I'll bring a book," Cara said. "We can even go to the library. I don't care, as long as we're together."

"OK. Come on up. I'll see you soon," Steven said. They said goodbye and Steven hung up the phone. He was not quite sure whether he felt more flattered or irritated. Cara was driving up to the university for the second night that week. It was a real turnaround. Before her trip to London, Cara had been acting distant and preoccupied, but since her return, she was more affectionate than ever. Steven smiled, remembering their reunion on Sunday night. They had driven his VW to Miller's Point, a popular hilltop parking spot overlooking Sweet Valley. The electricity between them had been incredible. It felt magical and new, the way it had when they had first fallen in love.

Steven ran a hand through his dark hair. Cara meant a lot to him, but so did his education. He couldn't afford to slack off now; he wouldn't have a prayer of getting accepted into the special law program if he did.

It seemed to Steven as if he had only just cracked his political science book when Cara knocked on the door of the living room he shared with his roommate, Bob Rose. "It's open," Steven yelled.

Before he could stand up, Cara dashed into his bedroom and wrapped her arms around his neck. "Hi there!" she said, showering his face with kisses.

Steven laughed. Twisting in his desk chair, he grabbed Cara and pulled her onto his lap. "What a reckless display of affection. You're lucky Bob's not around. He'd give us a hard time."

"I don't care *who* knows how much I love you," Cara replied. She kissed Steven again, this time more deeply.

"Whoa." Steven held her at arm's length and smiled. "This isn't a good way to start if we plan to get any work done. What are you going to read?"

Cara kissed him again. "I didn't bring a book."

"But I told you—" Steven swallowed his annoyance. "Here." He handed Cara a yellow legal pad. "You can write a letter or something. Didn't you say you owed Charlie a letter?"

Charlie was Cara's thirteen-year-old brother. After Mr. and Mrs. Walker's divorce, he had moved to Chicago with his father. "Yeah, I guess I do." Cara took the pad of paper reluctantly.

Her disappointment was impossible to miss. "Look, just for an hour, all right?" Steven said. "We'll still have time to talk before you go."

"OK." Cara stood up and went over to Steven's bed. She settled back against the pillows, the legal pad propped on her knees.

Steven turned back to his book. When he glanced over at Cara a few minutes later, he saw her staring at him instead of writing, an odd look in her dark eyes. "Writer's block?" Steven guessed. "Why don't you tell him what you did in London?"

A shadow flickered across Cara's face. She dropped her head and a curtain of long, shiny hair fell across her cheek. "Good idea," she murmured.

Steven tapped his fingers on his desk as he read. Cara's restlessness was contagious. It was hard to concentrate; he had a feeling she was still staring at him. Suddenly, Steven felt hands on his shoulders. He jumped. "Cara! What do you want?"

"I just want you," Cara whispered, nuzzling her face against his neck.

11

Steven closed his book. "I might as well face it," he grumbled. "I'm not going to get any work done tonight! Come on, let's go for a walk."

Outside, the moonlit campus was quiet. Steven slung an arm around Cara's shoulders as they strolled across the grassy quadrangle to a bench with a view of the dark mountains in the distance. They sat down, and Steven put a hand under Cara's chin and tilted her face to his for a kiss. But to his surprise, she pushed him away. Wasn't some romantic togetherness what Cara wanted tonight? "What's going on?" he asked her, beginning to get annoyed with Cara's erratic behavior.

In response, Cara put her hands to her face and burst into tears. Steven stared at her, astonished. Cara was sobbing uncontrollably. "Cara, what's wrong?" he demanded.

"Oh, Steven!" She continued to sob as he hugged her to him, stroking her damp cheek with his hand.

"Tell me, Cara," Steven insisted.

"My—mother," Cara began, her voice trembling with emotion.

The night air suddenly felt cold on Steven's skin. "Is she sick?"

Cara shook her head. "No, nothing like that. Her business trip . . . it wasn't an ordinary one."

"She didn't lose her job, did she?" Steven asked.

Again, Cara shook her head. "No. Worse than that."

What could be worse than that? Steven wondered.

Cara took a deep, shaky breath. She looked straight ahead at the line of the hills rather than at Steven. "The real reason we went to London was because Mom was being considered for a big promotion."

"Well, that's great. Isn't it?"

"You don't understand," she told him. "A promotion—and a transfer."

"A transfer?"

"They called her on Monday, after we got back to Sweet Valley. She got the job at the London office. She starts in less than three weeks." Cara's voice dropped to a whisper. "Steven, my mother and I—we're moving to London."

Slowly, Cara turned to face Steven. He stared back at her, but he couldn't speak or move his hands to touch her. It was as if the shock had drained all the power from his body, all the blood from his heart.

Finally, he managed to stutter, "You can't. You can't go."

"Do you think I want to?" Cara cried.

Steven reached for Cara. He held her as tightly as he could, but even so he felt as if she were already slipping through his fingers, leaving him. *You can't go*, he repeated silently. *Don't go. Don't leave me like Tricia did.*

When his former girlfriend, Tricia Martin,

had died of leukemia, Steven thought he would never get over the pain. It had taken a long time for him to feel that his life still had any purpose. It was Cara who had helped him to get over his loss, and in their time together Steven had grown to love Cara with even more depth and passion than he had felt for Tricia. And now he was going to lose Cara, too.

Steven stroked Cara's hair, her face, her shoulders, devouring her with his eyes, which, like hers, were filled with tears. "Cara," he whispered hoarsely. "Please don't leave me."

Cara looked at him helplessly. "Oh, Steven, what are we going to do?"

Two

"You knew about the possibility of your mom getting transferred *before* you went to London? And you didn't tell us? No wonder you weren't looking forward to the trip!" Amy commiserated as she wrapped a framed photograph of Cara and Steven in tissue paper and carefully placed it in a large cardboard box.

It was Saturday afternoon and Jessica, Amy, and Lila had come over to the fourth-floor apartment on Roundtree Road where Cara and her mother had lived since the Walkers' divorce. They were helping Cara pack some things that were to be shipped ahead to London. After telling Steven about the move Thursday night, Cara had realized she could not put off telling her friends any longer and had shared the sad news with them at school on Friday.

15

"The company sure didn't waste any time, and neither did your mom," Jessica observed. "I can't believe that in two and a half weeks you'll be in London for good!"

Cara couldn't believe it either. But it was real; it was happening.

"I'm glad my father runs his own company," Lila said. "Nobody can transfer *him*."

Jessica frowned at Lila. "Thanks for reminding us, Lila." She turned to Cara. "Tell us about your new apartment in London," she said.

"To tell you the truth, I don't remember it all that clearly," Cara admitted. She and her mother had looked at a number of flats while they were in London, and Mrs. Walker had since phoned the realtor to confirm a rental in the elegant neighborhood of Knightsbridge. But the whole process had been a blur to Cara. She hadn't wanted to see the apartments, or the city. She had even hoped that her mother would not get the promotion. "I *think* it has bay windows overlooking a park."

"It sounds pretty," Amy ventured.

"Well, it's not," Cara said sharply. "London is hideous. It's nothing like California. It rains all the time. I'm going to hate it!" Hot tears sprang to her eyes. Wiping them away with the sleeve of her T-shirt, Cara forced herself to laugh. "At least the apartment has a guest bedroom, so all of you can come and visit me."

16

"As soon as school gets out for the summer, I'll be there," Jessica promised.

Cara collapsed on a beanbag chair. She reached under the bed and pulled out a flat plastic box. "I can't believe all the junk that's piled up over the years," she said. She removed the lid and held up an old, dried-out corsage. "Look at this!"

"What dance was that from?" Jessica asked.

Cara studied the brown flowers, the faded ribbon. "Oh, I don't remember." She tossed the corsage back in the box. She didn't want to remember. It was too painful. Her mother was dragging her away from her friends, her town, her school, her boyfriend. Before long, memories would be all she had.

Lila reached into the box. "An invitation to a party at my house!" she said.

Cara smiled. "That was a great party. Remember? You had a live band. Steven and I danced the whole night!"

"I really should have another party soon," Lila remarked. "How about a party in your honor, a going-away party?"

Cara shook her head. "Thanks, Li, but I don't think I could take a scene like that." Her voice shook, tears threatening again. *I'm not going to cry*, she told herself silently. "It's going to be hard enough to say goodbye to everyone."

Jessica jumped up from her chair and crossed the room to give Cara a hug. "Oh, Cara, it's going to be so lonely in Sweet Valley without you. Don't move."

Cara laughed through her tears. "OK, Jess. If you say so, I won't go."

Jessica sniffled. "Seriously, isn't there *anything* you can do?"

"I wish!" Cara rubbed her forehead; she had had a tension headache for a week now. "But the plans are already set. Mom's contracted the movers and booked our flights. I'm going, whether I want to or not."

At that moment, there was a knock on Cara's bedroom door. "Yeah?" she called.

Mrs. Walker peered around the door. "Hi, girls. I just thought I'd see how you're doing. Can I bring you something to eat or drink? I've got cookies and fruit and some fresh-squeezed orange juice."

Cara was about to decline her mother's offer, but Amy spoke first. "That sounds great, Mrs. Walker. Can I help you?"

"No, I can get it." Mrs. Walker disappeared. A few minutes later, she returned with a tray. She lingered for a moment in the doorway, as if she might like to chat with the girls, but when Cara didn't look at her or speak to her, Mrs. Walker made a quiet exit.

"You're pretty mad at her, huh?" Jessica guessed, reaching hungrily for a plump, fuzzy peach.

"Why shouldn't I be?" Cara said defensively.

18

"If it weren't for her stupid job, this wouldn't be happening!"

"It's not a stupid job, though," Amy reminded her. "It's your mom's career. You should be proud of her, making a new life for herself."

"But what about *my* life?" Cara rejoined. "Doesn't it count for anything?"

Amy sighed. "You're right. It's really *not* fair. I remember how mad I was when we had to move from Vermont because WXAB offered my mom the sportscasting job."

"But that was different," Cara said. "You weren't moving to a strange new place a million miles away. You were moving back to the town where you were born!"

"But after all those years, Sweet Valley *was* like a new place," Amy persisted. "Everybody had grown up and changed. I had to make friends all over again."

"You'll make new friends in London," Jessica told Cara.

"But I don't *want* to make new friends." Cara yanked a tissue from the box and blew her nose. "I want to keep the friends I have."

"I didn't say you'd make friends as good as us," Jessica amended. "But, you know, just because you're moving doesn't mean we won't stay friends. I, for one, am not going to let little things like the continent of North America and the Atlantic Ocean come between us!"

Cara smiled weakly. She appreciated Jessica's

enthusiasm; she only wished she could share it. But she knew how expensive overseas phone calls were, and neither she nor Jessica were great letter writers. Sure, they would keep in touch for a while. But eventually other friends would fill Cara's place in Jessica's life. *And eventually another girl will take my place in Steven's heart.* That thought brought more tears to Cara's eyes, and she reached for another tissue.

Lila was reclining on Cara's bed. Now she sat up, but only to grab a cookie from the tray. "Well, if you really don't want to go to London, don't," she said, biting into the cookie for emphasis.

"I don't have a choice," Cara reminded her.

"Why can't you just live with your dad in Chicago?" Lila asked.

"Well, he hasn't invited me to," Cara answered.

"He probably assumes you're psyched about London," Jessica exclaimed. "I bet if you told him you aren't, he'd invite you to live with him and Charlie in Chicago."

Cara shrugged. "I don't know. Maybe. But it's kind of complicated." She shivered, recalling her parents' divorce and the arguments over where she and Charlie would live. Finally, the Walkers had compromised. Cara had stayed in Sweet Valley with their mother, and Charlie moved to Chicago with their dad. There had been no easy solution then and there was no easy solution now. In a way it would be great to live with her father and brother again, but

Cara knew that, as mad as she might be at the moment, she would miss her mother terribly if fhey were separated. *Why can't we just be a family the way we used to be?* Cara thought, not for the first time. *Mom and Dad and me and Charlie, all living together here in Sweet Valley. Why did everything have to change?*

"Anyway, it's not like Chicago is right down the road," she concluded out loud. "It's two thousand miles away. It wouldn't really be any better than London."

"I suppose you're right." Jessica sighed. "So much for that idea."

"I guess you just have to make the best of it," Amy said cheerfully as she sealed the cardboard box with heavy-duty tape. "It'll be hard at first, but after a while I bet you'll love London."

Cara shrugged. London might be glamorous and exciting, but it would never be *home*. Cara was overwhelmed by anger and frustration. She had absolutely no control over her own life! Her mother was hauling her off to London as if she were a suitcase instead of a person.

Make the best of it. . . . Cara threw a pile of paperback books into an empty box. She couldn't. She wouldn't.

It was a perfect night for dancing under the stars at the Beach Disco. The sky overhead was like a piece of black velvet scattered with sequins. But Steven was oblivious to the beauty of the setting. He was aware of only one person, one thing: the girl in his arms and the fact that soon she would be on a plane to London.

The current song had a quick-tempo, but Steven and Cara danced close and slowly. "Let's stay like this forever," Cara whispered, her breath warm against Steven's neck.

His arms tightened around her. "I wish we could," he whispered back.

He also wished they could leave the Beach Disco and go somewhere where they could be alone, but he knew Cara wanted to spend time with her other friends, too. There was so little time. Over Cara's head, Steven watched the people dancing near them. He glimpsed his sisters and their boyfriends. Jessica and Sam were laughing. Elizabeth and Todd were engaged in an animated discussion. Virtually everyone at the club looked carefree and happy. *Everyone but us . . .* Steven's jaw clenched. It simply wasn't fair.

"Remember our first date?" Cara said now, lifting sad but smiling eyes to Steven's.

He grinned. "Do I ever. I never expected to like you so much. I thought you were going to be a little too much like Jessica for my taste!"

Cara laughed. "Well, I *knew* I was going to fall for you. I'd admired you from afar for a long time."

"No, you didn't," Steven teased.

"Yes, I did," Cara insisted. "My best friend's

tall, dark, and handsome older brother, a sophisticated college man. How could I *not* have had a crush on you?"

"Well, when you put it that way . . ."

"Then I really got to know you," Cara continued, "and I found out that you weren't just handsome and smart, you were also the kindest, most wonderful guy in the whole world. . . ." Her voice cracked, and she hid her face against his broad chest. "I've never loved anyone the way I love you, Steven," she whispered.

Steven's throat tightened. "I love you, too, Cara."

"You'll forget all about me after a while."

"Never," he swore, his voice husky.

The song ended. Reluctantly, Steven and Cara stepped apart. Making a visible effort, she flashed him a bright smile. "I'm dehydrated from crying so much. How about getting something to drink?"

Together they walked toward the juice bar on the opposite side of the dance floor. While Cara ducked into the girls' room, Steven ordered two sodas.

Glasses in hand, he looked around for an empty table. Just then, Elizabeth appeared at his side. "Having fun?" she asked.

Steven shrugged. "I guess I'm having as much fun as I can, considering the fact that I'm absolutely miserable."

He rested the glasses on a nearby table. Elizabeth slipped an arm around her brother's waist. "I know how hard this is for you," she said softly. "I know what it's like, having to say goodbye to someone you love."

Steven looked down into his younger sister's sympathetic eyes. "That's right," he said. "I guess it was just as tough for you when Todd's dad was transferred to Burlington."

Elizabeth nodded. "When Todd moved away, I was crushed. I never *dreamed* we'd be reunited. But we were. Maybe someday you and Cara will be, too."

Steven looked skeptical. "How? When?"

"Well . . ." Elizabeth considered. "She could come back to California to go to college."

"She's just a junior. College is still a long way off," Steven said glumly.

"You can still hope, Steven," his sister said. "Maybe someday . . ."

Steven frowned. "Sorry, but I just don't believe in 'someday,' Liz. There wasn't any someday for me and Tricia, and there won't be one for me and Cara, either."

Elizabeth gasped. "Don't talk that way, Steven."

"Why not?"

"You sound so . . . so hopeless. So desperate!"

"Well, that's the way I feel," he declared roughly. "When Cara leaves, it will be forever."

Elizabeth wanted to reassure her brother, but there was nothing else she could say. She squeezed his arm and slipped away into the crowd.

His throat suddenly bone-dry, Steven gulped down his soda. He saw Cara approaching. She was smiling at her friends, trying so hard to be cheerful. Steven's heart ached. His own words echoed in his brain like a voice from a nightmare. It was inevitable. *When Cara leaves, it will be forever.*

In all his life, Steven had never felt so powerless. At least when Tricia had been near death, he had been able to accept the fact that her illness was beyond all human control. This was different. *I should be able to* do *something!* Steven thought desperately.

Three

"It *never* rains in southern California," Sam grumbled, looking out the window of the Wakefields' den at the steady downpour.

"Well, it's raining today," Jessica said, her eyes glued to the TV screen.

It was Sunday afternoon. Sam had dropped in on Jessica unexpectedly because his dirt bike rally had been canceled. He sat next to Jessica on the sofa, careful not to disturb the big bowl of popcorn she had balanced on her lap.

A commercial flashed on the screen and Jessica moved the popcorn to the end table so that she could wrap her arms around Sam. "I ordered this weather just to get you to hang out with *me* today, instead of with your dirt bike buddies," Jessica whispered.

"I guess this isn't so bad, afterall," Sam teased. He brushed a strand of golden hair back

26

from her forehead and gave her a lingering kiss. "Hmm, I kind of like that. I guess this isn't so bad at all."

He bent to kiss her again, but Jessica wriggled out of his grasp. The movie had resumed and she didn't want to miss a single second of it. Sam shook his head. "How can you stand to watch this corny old movie?" he asked, reaching over to grab a handful of popcorn.

"It's *not* corny. It's a classic," Jessica informed him. "It's the saddest and most romantic movie ever. Ryan O'Neal is so gorgeous, and Ali MacGraw is so tragically beautiful. . . ." Jessica reached for the box of tissues on the end table and positioned it on her lap. She had seen *Love Story* at least three or four times, and she knew she would need the tissues before long.

"It's just a movie," Sam reminded her.

"It may be just a movie, but it's a lot like real life. They're young and in love, and she's dying! How would you feel if *I* died?" she asked melodramatically.

"Don't even *say* such a thing!"

"Well, it could happen," Jessica insisted. "My brother had a girlfriend who died. So you'd better appreciate me while you have me!"

"I appreciate you plenty," Sam assured her.

The *Love Story* theme song swelled as the hero and heroine kissed. A tear trickled down Jessica's cheek as she thought of her brother and his tragic relationship with Tricia Martin.

Jessica had never been wild about Tricia, but she loved her brother dearly and she had shared in his pain.

"Poor Steven," she mused out loud. "Someone should make a movie about *him*. He's had so much tragedy in his love life. First Tricia dies and now Cara's moving halfway around the world."

"It is pretty rotten luck," Sam agreed.

Jessica wiped away another tear. There was no doubt about it. Steven and Cara's situation was dire. Cara's moving to London was almost as bad as if she were dying! Steven would never see Cara again. *And they're really in love. They might even have gotten married someday*, Jessica thought. At least the hero and heroine of *Love Story* had been married. They had been truly united, body and soul, before being parted forever.

Suddenly, Jessica sat bolt upright. That was it! The couple in *Love Story* were in college, not much older than Steven and Cara. Jessica shoved aside the box of tissues and jumped to her feet. "Where are you going?" Sam called after her as she bolted from the room. "You're going to miss the end of the movie!"

"I'll be back!" Jessica cried. Forget the end of the movie. *She* was interested in real life. And she had just discovered the perfect ending to Steven and Cara's real-life love story.

She ran up the stairs three at a time and skidded down the hall to Steven's bedroom. He was home for the weekend and was forcing

28

himself to spend a few hours apart from Cara in order to get some studying done.

Jessica burst into her brother's room without bothering to knock. Steven looked up from his book in surprise. "Steven, I've figured it all out!" she announced excitedly. "You and Cara don't have to break up."

"We don't?"

"No." Jessica flashed him a triumphant smile. "All you have to do is get married!"

Steven's eyes, already wide, grew even wider. "Get *what?*"

"Get married," Jessica repeated. "It's the perfect solution! You and Cara are in love, right? You'd probably get married someday, anyway. But if you get married *now*, Cara won't have to move to London with her mom. She'll stay in Sweet Valley with you. You'll be together forever!"

Steven sat back in his chair and stared up at Jessica. Jessica held her breath and watched her brother impatiently, waiting for him to consider her suggestion and discover that it was absolutely brilliant.

Slowly, a smile spread across Steven's face. He sat up straighter, as if an incredible burden had been lifted from his shoulders.

Steven jumped to his feet. "Why didn't *I* think of that?" he shouted. "Jess, you're a genius!"

Jessica grinned smugly. "No kidding."

Steven fumbled on top of his desk for his car

keys. He found them and stuck them in his pants pocket. Then, impulsively, he picked Jessica up by the waist and twirled her around. They were both laughing breathlessly. "I'm going to do it," he declared when he set her down again. "I'm going over to Cara's right now."

Jessica clapped her hands. "Good luck!" she called as Steven strode from the room.

Jessica collapsed backwards on Steven's bed. *I'm a genius!* she thought happily. Steven was on his way to Cara's to propose, and it was all Jessica's idea!

It was perfect. Steven would ask Cara to marry him and, of course, she would say yes. Instead of going to London with her mother, Cara would remain in Sweet Valley as Steven's wife and Jessica's good friend. *My friend and sister-in-law.* Steven and Cara's love wouldn't be sacrificed to circumstance after all. They would get married. In fact, they would probably elope! It would be incredibly romantic, even more romantic than a movie. *And it was all my idea!*

"Sure, come on up," Cara said over the intercom when Steven rang her from the foyer of the apartment building. She smiled as she waited for him. It was only four o'clock. So much for his vow that he would study until dinnertime. Fine with her. She was ready for a break after packing and cleaning all afternoon.

He rapped on the door. Cara opened it and then gasped. "Steven, is something wrong?"

Steven was breathless and soaked by the rain. "I came right over," he told her. "I didn't even think to bring a jacket or umbrella."

"What's so urgent?" she asked.

"This." Steven took her hand and led her to the living room couch. He sat down next to her, still holding her hand, his eyes intent on her face. "Cara, will you—" He broke off and glanced around the room. "Is your mom home?"

Cara was mystified by Steven's peculiar behavior. "No. Why?"

"Good." Steven slid off the sofa. He knelt on one knee and took both her hands now. Cara stared down at him. She couldn't remember ever hearing Steven's voice so serious. "Cara, will you marry me?"

I must be lightheaded from cleaning-fluid fumes, Cara thought wildly. "What did you say?"

"Will you marry me?" Steven repeated.

Cara was speechless. Steven was proposing to her! But could he actually be serious? Steven hurried to fill the silence. "I know this is kind of sudden," he apologized. "And I'm sorry I don't have a ring. I wish I could do it right."

Cara giggled. She couldn't help it; it had just struck her how funny they must look—her in a pair of dusty overalls and a T-shirt, her long hair tied back by a bandana, and Steven on his knees, dripping wet. "You—you're kidding, right?" she asked.

"No," Steven said. "I love you, Cara. I want to marry you."

Cara searched his face. His expression was earnest and passionate. No, he wasn't kidding. Suddenly Cara felt weak, and she sank back against the couch. She knew she was supposed to say something now, but she just couldn't remember *what*. How did characters in books and movies react to marriage proposals?

I'm supposed to answer him. Yes or no.

"I know this is unexpected," Steven said again. His tone was patient and reassuring.

Cara relaxed. "Yeah, it really is."

"You don't have to answer this minute."

Cara tugged on Steven's hand, pulling him up onto the sofa beside her. "Steven, you know I love you," she said. "With all my heart. But getting married—" She stopped. Would he be offended if she confessed she had never even *thought* about marriage? She loved Steven more than anyone she had ever dated, but getting married was something other people did, other *older* people. *Much* older people.

And getting married wasn't something that should be done on a whim, either. Cara knew that many marriages ended in divorce; her own parents' had. "Steven, this is crazy," she finally said. "You're a freshman in college. And I'm still in high school! We haven't even been seeing each other that long. Of course I love you, but—"

"I knew you'd think I was out of my mind,"

Steven interrupted. "I wish we could do it the usual way—go out for a few years, graduate from college, and then get married. But we can't. We don't have time."

Cara shivered. The truth of what Steven said was like an icy grip around her heart. *Mom and I are leaving for London in just a few weeks . . . There's no time . . .* "We don't have time, but we still have to think carefully about this," she protested.

"I *have* thought about it." Steven grinned. "On the way over here in the car! Listen, Cara. It's the only way for us to stay together. It's the only way for you to stay in Sweet Valley. Isn't that what you want?"

"Yes, but—"

"Oh, Cara, it will be wonderful." Steven enveloped her in a loving embrace. "We'll find a little apartment of our own, right here in Sweet Valley! After you finish high school, we'll move up closer to the university. We'll help each other through college. It won't be easy, but I can get a part-time job. We'll get by. We'll have each other."

Cara's eyes filled with tears as she listened to the tender, romantic picture Steven painted. "A little apartment," she whispered. She imagined inviting Jessica and her other friends over for parties. They could make all the noise they wanted, stay up as late as they pleased! It would be *Cara's* own apartment, not her mother's. And Steven . . . There weren't many men like Steven. He was loving, honest, and strong, someone she could lean on, depend on. Steven would never let her down.

"Oh, Steven," Cara whispered. She put her hands to his face, brushing the damp hair back from his forehead. "I love you so much. I want to be with you. But are you sure?"

"I've never been more sure of anything," Steven declared. "But *you* have to be sure, too. It's your life, Cara."

"My life," she said softly. Then she repeated the words with more conviction. "Yes, it's my life."

It *was* her life, and she had the right to do whatever she wanted with it. Lately, she had been feeling so helpless, as if she were being swept along by events over which she had no control. But it didn't have to be that way. She was old enough to make her own decisions about how and where she would live her life.

And I want to live with Steven, Cara decided. *I want to live in Sweet Valley.* Getting married wasn't such a crazy idea after all; it was her chance to take her life back into her own hands. "Say we decide to get married," Cara began.

Steven's eyes lit up. "Is that a yes?" he asked eagerly.

She laughed. "It's almost a yes," she promised. "But it's one thing to talk about it. How do we actually *do* it? When and where, and what are we going to tell our parents?"

"I don't think we should tell them anything,

not until after the fact," Steven said. Cara nodded in agreement. "And how about two weekends from now, the Saturday before your mom leaves for London?" Cara nodded again. "As for the rest," Steven concluded, "I'll take care of all the details. All you'll have to do is come with me to the church and say 'I do.' "

Cara's eyes filled again with tears. "If you want to ask your question again, I think I'm ready with my answer," she said softly.

Steven put his arms around her. "Cara Walker, will you marry me?" he asked solemnly.

"Yes," she whispered.

As Steven's lips met hers in a deep kiss, the words she would speak in two weeks' time repeated themselves in Cara's head like notes of beautiful music. *I do, I do, I do . . .*

Four

After seeing Steven off on his romantic mission, Jessica hurried back to the den and switched off the TV set. "Hey," Sam protested. "The movie's not over yet!"

"Sorry. But something's come up. Something *very* important."

"What?"

"I can't tell you. Not yet, anyway." Jessica gave Sam a quick kiss, grabbed his hands, hauled him to his feet, and propelled him toward the door. "Here's your jacket. Call me tonight, OK? Bye!"

With Sam out of the way, Jessica immediately got on the telephone. By the time she heard Steven's car in the driveway, she had done a lot of research. Oblivious to the rain, Jessica rushed outside to meet her brother. "What did she say?" she squealed, unable to bear the suspense a moment longer. "What are you doing back so soon? Don't tell me she said—"

"Her mom came home, so I left. Cara's meeting me at the Box Tree Café later." Steven's goofy grin gave him away. "She said yes!"

"All right!" Jessica threw herself on Steven, and the two spun around in a dizzy victory dance. But Jessica didn't want to waste too much time. "Come on," she said to Steven. "Let me tell you what I found out while you were gone."

"Is anyone else home?" Steven asked as they entered the kitchen together.

"Nope. Mom and Dad were planning to get an early dinner after the matinee, and Liz is still at Todd's. Here, check this out!"

She directed Steven's attention to a pad of paper on which she had scribbled the addresses of half a dozen marriage chapels in Nevada. "As far as I can tell, these towns are the closest. I called each of the chapels, and you won't believe how easy it's going to be! All you need are the rings and a blood test. They'll take care of all the details. You can even *rent* flowers!"

"Wow." Steven sank into a chair at the table. "That's a little scary. It's almost too easy!"

"Well, we're not done yet," Jessica reminded him. "Here." She pushed the Sweet Valley telephone book at him. "Let's look up jewelers in the Yellow Pages."

Steven did not move. Jessica pulled the

phone book back and quickly flipped through the pages. "I'd try North's Jewelry Store in the mall. Their prices are reasonable. You'd better call first thing tomorrow to order the rings," she directed.

"The rings. Yeah, sure," Steven agreed, sounding dazed.

"Steven, wake up!" Jessica exclaimed. "Aren't you excited?"

Steven smiled groggily. "Yeah, of course. My head's still kind of spinning, that's all."

Jessica dropped into another chair. "So, tell me everything. How did you ask her? Where were you? What did she do?"

Steven recapped the scene for Jessica. "It probably wasn't the most romantic proposal ever," he conceded. "But it felt pretty good to me."

"It sounds like a *perfect* proposal," Jessica declared. "You and Cara are going to be so happy!"

Steven tilted his head. "Yeah, I suppose we will."

"So, when's the date?"

"A week from Saturday, three days before she's supposed to go to London with her mom."

"That gives us plenty of time to arrange everything," Jessica said confidently.

"I suppose it does. But one thing, Jess. No one else can know about this. No one but you and me and Cara. And I didn't tell her this whole thing was really your idea, but I did tell her you and I had talked it over."

"We have to maintain absolute secrecy," Jessica agreed emphatically. "This is so exciting!"

"Cara and I decided we'll tell people we're going on a ski trip with some of my college friends that weekend. That way we can disappear for a couple of days without anyone getting suspicious."

Jessica nodded. "It's a great plan."

"I guess we'll have to come back to Sweet Valley sometime on Sunday to break the news that we're married," Steven concluded.

"Everyone will be really happy about it, once they get used to the idea," Jessica said encouragingly.

"Not Mom and Dad." Steven grimaced. "They're going to kill me."

Jessica wrinkled her nose. "Maybe they'll want to, but it will be too late for them to do anything about it, right?"

"Right."

"So, it's settled then. You and Cara are getting married!" It was such wonderful news. It was going to be agonizing to keep it all to herself. "Are you sure I can't tell anyone?" Jessica asked. "Not even Sam?"

"Not even Sam," Steven insisted. "We just can't risk the possibility of the news getting back to Cara's mother or Mom and Dad."

"And I can't tell Liz?"

"Definitely not Liz!"

Jessica considered this and quickly saw that Steven was right. Cautious, practical Elizabeth would *never* approve of something as wild and crazy as an elopement. "She'd try to talk you out of it," Jessica said.

"Maybe worse," said Steven. "She might even feel obligated to tell Mom and Dad, who'd definitely try to stop the whole thing."

"No, Elizabeth can't find out," Jessica concluded.

"That means *you* have to keep your mouth shut." As Steven studied his younger sister, Jessica tried her best to appear entirely reliable. "Can you do that?" he asked.

"Of course I can!" Jessica folded her arms across her chest. "I can't believe you, Steven. Give me some credit! Whose idea was this, anyway? I'd think you'd be a little more grateful!"

"You're right." He grinned. "Sorry. It's just that I know you and Liz are used to telling each other pretty much everything."

"Believe me, there's lots I don't tell Liz," Jessica informed him. "You and Cara can trust me. My lips are sealed!"

Monday at school, Cara was quiet and distracted. She had hardly slept a wink the night before. She had just become engaged! Who could sleep under such circumstances? Instead, she had lain awake for hours, remembering Ste-

ven's every word, every gesture, the ___
eyes as he had asked her to marry h___
had never felt so sure of Steven's love
devotion, and her own love for him had nev___
been stronger. The idea of eloping and con-
fronting her mother with the news that she
would not be accompanying her to London was
daunting; Cara was glad she had almost two
weeks to get her nerve up. But it would all
work out, and in the end she would have what
she wanted: Steven, and a life of her own in
Sweet Valley.

Now, as she deposited her lunch tray at a
table with Jessica, Lila, and Amy, Cara had to
bite her lip to keep from smiling. As she sat
down she caught Jessica's eye. Jessica winked
broadly. Cara giggled.

"What's so funny?" asked Amy as she forked
into her chef's salad.

"Nothing." Cara pretended to be intent on
unwrapping her turkey sandwich.

"Cara's just a little nervous," Jessica remarked knowingly.

"Nervous about what?" Lila asked.

"About moving to London," Cara said quickly.
"Wouldn't you be?"

"No," Lila replied. "I'd love to live abroad in
a sophisticated city instead of in this boring little town."

"Well, I like it here," said Cara. "I don't
think there could be anyplace on earth I'd like
as much."

ıy sighed. "It's so sad that you have to leave."

Cara tried her hardest to look glum. "I know."

She bit into her sandwich and looked anxiously at Jessica. What were the odds, Cara wondered, that Jessica, the world's worst secret-keeper, would be able to keep *this* secret for two whole weeks? What were the odds that she would be able to keep it for two whole *minutes*?

"Well, Cara, you don't really *have* to leave Sweet Valley," Jessica said suddenly.

"She doesn't?" Amy asked.

"What she means is that my heart will always stay in Sweet Valley. And I can always come back and visit. Right, Jessica?" Cara stretched her leg under the table and gave Jessica a sharp kick.

"Right," Jessica agreed quickly. "That's exactly what I meant."

Cara frowned. It had been going on like this all day. Jessica was always on the verge of giving it all away. When they met in the locker room after school to change for cheerleading practice, Cara dragged Jessica to a quiet corner. "Jess, would you stop it?" she hissed.

"Stop what?" Jessica asked.

"Will you get off the subject of my moving, or rather my *not* moving? Someone's going to guess what's going on!"

"I'm trying," Jessica swore. "I haven't actually told anybody, have I?"

"Not in so many words," Cara conceded.

"But that doesn't mean it's not completely obvious that you have some big news."

"Relax," Jessica advised. "Your secret is safe with me. I won't give you away."

"You'd better not." Cara put her hands on her hips. "I'm serious, Jessica. Steven and I can't pull this off if word gets out. We're counting on you."

"You can trust me," Jessica promised.

Five minutes later they joined the rest of the Sweet Valley High cheerleading squad in the gym. "What's up, Jessica?" her co-captain, Robin Wilson, asked as soon as they appeared.

"Nothing's up," Jessica replied. "*I'm* not up to anything!" she added with a hard-to-miss glance in Cara's direction.

Cara sighed. *Here we go again!*

"What's up, Jess?" Elizabeth asked that evening when Jessica strolled into the kitchen.

"Why does everybody keep asking me what's up?" Jessica demanded. "What could possibly be up?"

Elizabeth calmly continued to stir the pasta sauce. "It's just an expression. Let me try again. Hi, Jess! What's new?"

"Nothing's new," Jessica insisted. "What could possibly be new?"

"I don't know." Elizabeth added some black pepper to the sauce. "You tell me."

"I'm not telling you anything," Jessica replied.

"So, you *do* have something to tell!" Elizabeth declared triumphantly.

Jessica looked disconcerted, and Elizabeth laughed. Jessica was as transparent as glass. Jessica was hiding something, and sooner or later, Elizabeth would get the scoop. It was just a question of how long Jessica could hold out.

"All right, spill the beans," Elizabeth ordered. Jessica edged toward the door. "Not so fast! Here, taste this. Does it need more seasoning?"

Jessica tasted the sauce. "Umm." She took another spoonful. "This is great!"

Elizabeth grabbed Jessica and pinned her against the counter. "So, what's the gossip?"

Jessica wriggled out of Elizabeth's grasp. "There isn't any! And it doesn't have anything to do with Steven, either!"

"Steven, huh?" Elizabeth quickly considered what might be newsworthy about her brother. She hadn't seen much of him lately; he had been home for the weekend, but he had spent most of his time either studying or with Cara. Elizabeth continued to think rapidly. She could pinpoint exactly when Jessica had started acting funny. It had been the night before. Steven had gone out to eat with Cara, but first he had sat for a while at the dinner table with his family. When Steven had announced that he was planning a ski trip to the mountains with Cara and some of his friends from college the weekend before Cara was scheduled to move to England,

44

Jessica had started to giggle. Then she had choked on her soda and had had to leave the table.

"Does this have anything to do with Steven's ski trip?" Elizabeth asked.

Jessica's eyes grew as wide as saucers. Clapping a hand over her mouth, she bolted from the kitchen.

Elizabeth shook her head. Her curiosity was definitely aroused, but if the past was anything to go by, she knew it wouldn't be long before it was satisfied. Jessica Wakefield subscribed to the theory that secrets were no fun unless shared.

After school on Tuesday, Elizabeth made herself comfortable at the study table in her bedroom. "Eyes and Ears," her weekly gossip column for the school newspaper, was due Wednesday. Elizabeth tapped her pencil on the tabletop. There didn't seem to be very much going on at Sweet Valley High these days. Of course, Cara was moving to London, but that was about it. Too bad she hadn't already figured out what Jessica was hiding!

The phone on her night table rang and Elizabeth crossed the room to answer it. "Hello," she said.

"May I speak to Steven Wakefield?" a woman's voice asked.

"He's not here, but I could get a message to him," Elizabeth offered.

"Thanks. Would you ask him to give Barbara at North's Jewelry Store a call?"

"North's Jewelry Store?" Elizabeth repeated. *Steven's probably buying Cara a special going-away present*, she guessed.

"That's right." The woman recited the store's phone number, and Elizabeth jotted it down. "I have a question about the engraving on the wedding rings he ordered yesterday."

Elizabeth froze, her fingers tightening around the pencil. *Wedding rings?* "Steven Wakefield ordered wedding rings?"

"That's right."

"I'll give him the message," Elizabeth promised weakly. She replaced the receiver, then collapsed on her bed, her head spinning. Steven had ordered wedding rings! If Jessica knew about this, it would certainly explain her secretive mood.

Steven and Cara were planning to get married! "Has he gone absolutely crazy?" Elizabeth wondered out loud. He must have. Why else would he have given the jewelry store his home number and not his number at the dorm? Elizabeth put her hands to her head. She knew her brother was torn up over the prospect of being parted from Cara. But it had never occurred to her that Steven loved Cara enough to ask her to marry him now.

Maybe I'm overreacting, Elizabeth thought. Steven had ordered rings, but that didn't necessarily mean he and Cara were getting married right away. They simply couldn't be. "Maybe they aren't even wedding rings," Elizabeth said aloud. "Maybe they're more like friendship rings. That wouldn't be so bad."

Elizabeth stood up. She knew she wouldn't have to wait too much longer to get answers to her questions. Jessica would be home from cheerleading practice any minute now.

Elizabeth was waiting for her twin at the door when Jessica breezed in, a gym bag slung over her shoulder. "Hi, Liz!" she said. And then she stopped. Elizabeth was blocking her path, a very serious expression on her face.

"Uh-oh," Jessica said.

"What's going on with Steven and Cara?" Elizabeth demanded.

"What do you mean?" Jessica asked innocently.

"I mean that I just took a call from North's Jewelry Store, and apparently Steven has ordered wedding rings! What's going on?"

"I don't know anything about it," Jessica declared. "Maybe the store made a mistake."

"It wasn't a mistake and you know it," Elizabeth said. "If you don't tell me what this is all about, I'm going to ask Steven himself."

"Well, OK," Jessica said. Her eyes sparkled. Elizabeth bet Jessica was glad her twin had found out. She must have been dying to tell someone the news.

The twins sat down at the butcher block

table. Jessica took a deep, dramatic breath and announced, "Steven and Cara are getting married!"

Elizabeth sank back in her chair. So it was true! "When?" she asked. "Where?"

"A week from Saturday," Jessica replied. "The ski trip is just a cover. They're really going to drive to Nevada, to elope! Isn't it exciting?"

"Exciting?" Elizabeth stared at her twin. "You've got to be kidding!"

"Of course it's exciting. Just think—Cara will be our sister-in-law. Isn't that wonderful?"

"No, it's not wonderful," Elizabeth said.

Jessica narrowed her eyes. "Don't you dare tell Mom and Dad."

"I . . . I won't," Elizabeth said.

"Don't you dare," Jessica repeated firmly. "Steven has a right to make his own decisions, Liz. They'd only try to interfere."

"But maybe somebody *should* interfere," Elizabeth said. "It doesn't seem to me that Steven could have thought this through very thoroughly."

"He's thought about it plenty," Jessica stated. "He and Cara are going to get married so they won't have to be separated. Steven knows what he's doing. So don't tell Mom and Dad. Don't let Steven down."

Elizabeth nodded reluctantly. Steven was an adult. It was his prerogative not to discuss everything he did with his parents. Still,

Elizabeth was having a hard time getting over her astonishment, and her concern. "How are they going to support themselves? Steven's just a student. He doesn't have any money. Where are they going to live? And Cara's still in high school. How is she—"

"Don't be such a wet blanket," Jessica interrupted. "They'll make it work somehow. Love conquers all, right?"

"Love doesn't buy groceries. Love doesn't get you through college."

"You're so depressing!" Jessica complained. "Why can't you get just a *little* excited about the wedding and Steven's happiness?"

Elizabeth stifled a troubled sigh. "I only wish I could."

Five

"I'm starving," Cara declared as she scanned the menu. "We have absolutely no food in the house. My mom's so busy planning the move, she's forgotten that we need to eat. I think I could devour a Guido's special all by myself!"

Jessica glanced across the booth at Cara. It was Tuesday night and she, Amy, and Lila had met at Guido's Pizza Palace. Jessica wanted to tell Cara about the confrontation she had had with Elizabeth that afternoon, but so far she hadn't had a chance to talk to her alone. Now, after determining that Lila and Amy were intent on their menus, Jessica held her own menu up to her face as a shield. "Liz knows," she whispered to Cara.

Sharp-eared Lila looked up from her menu. "Knows what?"

Jessica opened her mouth, ready to lie to Lila.

Then she reconsidered. After all, she had already spilled the beans to Elizabeth. What harm could there be in telling a few more friends? Anyway, it would probably be better for Cara if more people knew. Amy and Lila would definitely support her. Besides, Jessica was just plain tired of keeping the secret.

Before Cara could stop her, Jessica blurted out the news. "Liz knows that Cara and Steven are planning to elope!"

Lila dropped her menu.

"What?" Amy squeaked.

"They're eloping. Getting married!" Jessica said loudly.

"Shhh!" Cara hissed.

"They're getting married," Jessica repeated in a whisper.

"Cara, that's wonderful!" Amy reached across the booth to take Cara's hand. "Congratulations!"

"When did this happen? How come I wasn't informed?" Lila demanded.

Cara laughed. "Only two days ago. Don't worry, Li. No one else knows besides you three and Elizabeth."

"Does this mean—does this mean you're staying in Sweet Valley instead of moving to London with your mother?" Amy asked.

Cara nodded, her smile widening. "Oh, Cara, I'm so glad!" Amy cried.

"Enough gushing," Lila said. "Let's hear the details. Did he ask you or did you ask him? And why don't you have an engagement ring?"

"He asked me. It was kind of spontaneous, so he didn't have time to buy a ring. And I don't want him to," Cara added. "We'll both wear wedding bands, and I think that's enough."

"You're not *really* engaged if you don't have a diamond," Lila said decidedly. "No man's marrying *me* until I have a big fat rock on my finger."

"Well, that sort of thing's just not important to me or to Steven," Cara told her. "What matters is that we love each other and that we want to make a life together."

Amy's eyes glistened with sentimental tears. "It's so romantic, I can't stand it!"

"I guess it *is* pretty romantic, ring or no ring," Lila conceded. "I've got to give you credit, Cara. I would never have thought you'd do such a wild thing!"

"It's not that wild, is it?" Cara asked anxiously.

"Are you kidding?" said Lila. "You'll be the only married woman in the Sweet Valley High junior class!"

"Will you stay in school?" Amy wondered.

"Of course I'll stay in school!" Cara cried. "And so will Steven. Nothing's going to change. We'll just be . . . married, that's all."

"It'll be a blast," said Jessica. "Your own apartment, no parents around to give you a curfew and then ground you if you stay out late. And you can eat whatever you want. Pizza every night!"

Cara smiled. "I hadn't thought about that particular advantage."

"Won't you miss your mom, though?" Amy asked after they had given their order to the waiter.

Cara shrugged. "Maybe a little. But in a year I would have left home to go to college. I'll visit her—" Cara corrected herself. "*We'll* visit her at some point."

Amy shook her head. "This is really unbelievable. I mean, it's great! But I guess I'm glad Barry and I are still years and years away from talking about marriage."

"Same goes for me and Sam," Jessica agreed.

"Thanks a lot, guys!" Cara exclaimed. "So being married is a fate worse, than death?"

"That's not what we meant and you know it," Amy said. "I'm incredibly happy for you. I think it's fantastic that you've found the person you want to spend the rest of your life with. But the rest of your life is a long time, and I know *I'm* not ready to make a decision like that. That's all."

Cara's forehead creased in a thoughtful frown. Her frown deepened when Lila said, "The rest of your life. Ugh!"

"Cara's the luckiest girl on earth!" Jessica protested. "It just so happens that the man she's going to spend the rest of her life with is my older brother, who, after myself, and Elizabeth, I admire more than anyone."

"Steven *is* special," Amy agreed.

A smile tugged at the corners of Cara's mouth. "Yeah, he is," she said softly.

There was a brief lull in the conversation when the pizzas arrived, and then the girls returned to the stimulating topic of Cara's engagement. "How are we going to celebrate?" Lila asked.

"We can't celebrate, at least not until after the wedding," Cara said.

"I wish you were having a *real* wedding so we could be bridesmaids," Amy said wistfully. "I don't suppose you want us tagging along with you to Nevada."

Cara laughed. "No, thanks. I don't think you're supposed to bring your friends along when you elope."

"Well, we have to do *something* for you," insisted Lila. "Just because you're eloping doesn't mean you should be completely deprived. We can at least *try* to do things right. I know! I'll give you a bridal shower."

Cara giggled. "A bridal shower?"

"It's traditional," Lila explained in a patronizing tone. "How about the day after tomorrow?"

"What fun!" Amy exclaimed.

"Well, OK, but it has to be a *secret* bridal shower," said Cara.

"No problem," said Lila. "No one's ever home but me and the house staff. It'll be very secret."

"It's the least we can do," Jessica agreed. And then, to her surprise, Cara's eyes suddenly brimmed with tears. "Thanks, you guys. I guess I'm glad you have the biggest mouth in town, Jess. I'm glad you all know."

"We're with you all the way," Amy assured her.

"That makes a big difference," Cara said.

Jessica helped herself to a huge slice of pepperoni pizza. She felt incredibly pleased with herself. Steven had almost blown it by giving the jewelry store the wrong phone number. It was fortunate that Elizabeth had taken the call, instead of one of their parents. But now everything was back on track. Everything was just fine.

"I'm eating dinner out, too," Elizabeth told Mrs. Wakefield after Jessica left for Guido's in Lila's lime-green Triumph.

"That's fine." Mrs. Wakefield opened the refrigerator and removed a Tupperware container. "I'm just reheating some of that great pasta sauce you made last night. Are you seeing Todd?"

"Actually, I'm meeting Steven," Elizabeth replied.

"Really? What's the occasion?"

Elizabeth jingled the keys to the Fiat, wishing she didn't have to lie to her mother. She didn't have a choice, though; she had promised Jessica she wouldn't reveal Steven's secret. "He—

he checked a couple of books out of the university library for me, some books I couldn't find at school. I need them for a history project."

"Well, give him a kiss from me. See you later."

Elizabeth had an hour's drive, during which she could contemplate her position. Steven wasn't actually meeting her tonight. He wasn't even expecting her. She had picked up the phone to call him, and then had hung up without dialing. She still wasn't sure what she wanted to say to him. She had to say *something*. She wasn't going to tell her parents—she had finally agreed with Jessica on that point—but she *did* want to make sure her brother knew what he was doing. Elizabeth couldn't help but feel that Steven and Cara were acting out of desperation rather than out of a real desire to spend the rest of their lives together.

Elizabeth rolled down her window, letting the wind ruffle her hair. Maybe it was none of her business. She tried to imagine how she would feel if their roles were reversed, if she and Todd were the ones planning to elope. Would she be offended if Steven tried to talk her out of it? Probably a little. But she'd also probably be grateful that her brother cared enough about her to risk her anger.

We have to talk this over together, Elizabeth thought with fresh determination. She and Steven were very close; they had been helping each other out with problems, big and small, for years. Elizabeth respected Steven's opinion immensely, and she knew he respected hers as well. Yes, she owed it to him.

Elizabeth parked the car on the quadrangle in front of Steven's dorm. She hoped her brother was studying in his room this evening rather than at the library. To her relief, Steven himself yelled, "Come on in!" when she knocked on his door.

He was standing in the living room weighing a big textbook in each hand. Elizabeth laughed. "Trying to figure out which one's heavier so you can read the other?" she guessed.

Steven grinned. "Something like that. Hey, what brings you up here?"

"Well . . ." Was it better to lead into the topic of the elopement gradually or should she get right to the point? Elizabeth decided to be up front with her brother. "Actually, I have a message for you. I took a phone call for you today. From North's Jewelry Store."

"Really?" Steven sat down at his desk. Elizabeth sat down on the couch. "What did they have to say?"

"You need to call Barbara at the store about the engraving on the wedding rings."

Sister and brother looked at each other for a moment without speaking. Elizabeth studied Steven's face, trying to read his emotions. Was he angry that she had found out? Was he relieved, maybe even glad that now he could be honest with her? It was impossible to tell; Steven's expression was neutral, masklike.

"Well, thanks for the message," he said at last. "I've got a lot of studying to do now. . . ." He turned away from Elizabeth and began to flip through the pages of a textbook.

This isn't going to be easy, Elizabeth realized. "Steven, I know what you and Cara are planning. Jessica told me."

"So why are you here?" Steven asked, his eyes on his book. "You know all there is to know."

Elizabeth bit her lip. "I just thought maybe you'd want to talk, that's all. Steven, have you really thought this through? I mean, getting married isn't something you do on the spur of the moment. Don't you think you might just be reacting to circumstances?"

Steven laughed dryly. "I knew there was a good reason why Jessica and I were going to keep you out of this. So, have you told Mom and Dad yet?"

"Of course not!" Elizabeth said, slightly offended. "And I'm not going to. I just want to help. I'm not criticizing you, Steven."

Steven's expression softened. "Well, thanks, I guess. But I don't need any help. Cara and I have made a decision. We're getting married. It's *our* business."

"Have you told anyone besides Jessica? What about Bob?" Steven's roommate, Bob, was a sensible guy, Elizabeth thought. He would be sure to try to talk Steven out of his plan. "I bet he'd be glad to give you advice."

"Look, Liz," Steven said bluntly. "I don't *need* advice—not yours, not Bob's, not anybody's. I've made up my mind and that's that. So let's drop it, OK?"

Elizabeth stood up. They weren't getting anywhere. Steven wasn't interested in what she had to say, at least not that night. She hoped his feelings would change but until they did, she might as well talk to a stone wall.

At the door, Elizabeth paused and looked back at her brother. The fat textbook on his desk reminded her of something else. "What about the special law program you've applied to?" she asked. "How can you do the extra work if you're married to Cara?"

From Steven's pained expression, Elizabeth could see that she had touched a raw nerve. Steven shook his head. "I won't get accepted," he said flatly, as if he were trying to convince himself as much as his sister. *He knows he can't do both, so he doesn't want to get accepted,* Elizabeth recognized dismally. *After all his hard work . . .* It was painfully clear. Steven was hoping he wouldn't have to choose between Cara and his career.

Without another word to her brother, Elizabeth stepped out into the hallway and pulled the door shut behind her.

Six

As she approached the driveway of Fowler Crest on Thursday afternoon, Cara fought back the urge to drive right past it. A bridal shower. She shivered. It would be too weird. The only bridal showers she had ever gone to had been for women much older than herself. Her mother had given one a few months earlier for a colleague from work, a woman in her thirties; Cara had also attended a shower for her cousin, a medical student in her mid-twenties. *I'm much too young for his kind of thing*, Cara thought. *I'm going to feel ridiculous.*

There were a number of cars parked in Lila's driveway, more than Cara had expected to see given the fact that it was supposed to be a very small party—just Lila, Jessica, and Amy, the only people who knew about her engagement. Cara killed the engine and stepped reluctantly from her mother's car. She knew she should be touched that her friends wanted to make a fuss over her. But she didn't want them to. It made the whole thing seem too—*real*.

At the same time, Cara welcomed the diversion. A party was better than another afternoon alone at home, pretending to sort through her things in order to pack for London, when she was really considering what to take with her to the apartment she would share with Steven after the wedding. If she was alone this afternoon, she would only think about the wedding and get scared.

It *had* seemed like a game at first, talking with Steven about setting up house. But over the past few days, vague misgivings had begun to creep into Cara's heart. She loved Steven more than ever. She was absolutely certain about that. And every night, when she saw Steven at the university or in Sweet Valley or talked with him on the phone, Cara's doubts faded away. But as soon as she was by herself again, the doubts returned, each time stronger than the time before. Cara could not forget what Amy had said at Guido's the other night. *The rest of your life . . . the rest of your life . . .* Cara loved Steven, but the more she considered the idea of marriage, the more she realized what an enormous step it was. Maybe she *wasn't* ready.

Cara squelched this thought as she walked up the path to the front door of the Spanish-style mansion. *Why are you being so negative?*

she chided herself. She and Steven got along so well. They loved each other so much. How could she doubt for a minute that they would live happily ever after? *Being married won't be all that different from going steady,* Cara decided hopefully as she pressed the bell.

Lila herself opened the door. As Cara stepped inside, Lila yelled over her shoulder. "Hey, everybody! The bride's here!"

Cara winced. "Do you have to call me that?"

"It's what you are, isn't it?"

Lila took Cara's arm and pulled her down the hallway. They rounded a corner, stopping at the entrance to the spacious Fowler Crest living room. "Surprise!" a chorus of voices greeted Cara.

Surprise was right. The living room was beautifully decorated with vases of pink and white roses and silver balloon bouquets. A pile of brightly wrapped gifts sat on the coffee table. But the decor was not what arrested Cara's attention. It was the group of girls looking at her. With Jessica and Amy were Robin, Maria Santelli, Rose Jameson, Sandra Bacon, and Jean West.

"It wasn't going to be much of a party with just the four of us," Jessica explained.

"We won't tell a soul," Maria promised.

As the girls clustered around to hug and congratulate her, Cara laughed. "Really, what did I expect?" she said ruefully. "Letting Jessica in on a secret is the best way to make sure everyone in Sweet Valley hears about it!''

"I've been very disciplined this time," Jessica defended herself. "I've only told—" she counted on her fingers, "eight people. Pretty good, considering I could have told eighty!"

"Thanks," said Cara dryly.

"OK, everybody. Eat," Lila ordered.

Cara admired the elegant display of breads, salads, and sweets. "Everything looks delicious."

"It had better be," said Lila carelessly. "I had it catered by Palomar House, one of *the* most elegant and expensive restaurants in Sweet Valley."

"This is wonderful, Lila," said Cara. "You didn't have to go to so much trouble."

"It's not every day one of your closest friends gets married," Lila pointed out.

Cara nodded as she filled her plate. As soon as she sat down on the couch Jessica thrust a package at her. "Let's open the presents," Jessica suggested. "I can't wait any longer!"

Cara smiled and put aside her plate. "Are all these for me? This is better than Christmas."

Cara slipped the small card out of the envelope that was attached to the package Jessica had handed her. "It's from Jessica, obviously," she told the others. "It says, 'To my future sister-in-law, with love.' " Cara's voice trembled with emotion.

"Don't cry," Jessica begged, her own eyes

bright with tears. "We're supposed to be laughing!"

Cara unwrapped the present. It was a video-tape of the movie *Barefoot in the Park*. "It's about these newlyweds, played by Robert Redford and Jane Fonda," Jessica explained. "They have some silly fights while they're getting used to living together but mostly they're just madly in love and . . . well, I hope that's the way it will be with you and Steven."

Cara smiled. "Thanks, Jessica. I can't wait to watch it with Steven. Now if we only had a TV and a VCR!"

"Well, don't look at me," said Lila. "I'm not *that* rich!" She tossed a box tied with a big silver bow at Cara. "Here, open this one next."

Cara read the name of the store printed on the box. "It's from Bibi's." There were oohs and ahs from the girls; Bibi's was an exclusive bou-tique at the Valley Mall.

Lila smirked. "I hope it fits."

Cara removed the lid from the box and pushed back the tissue paper. Inside was a diaphanous, lace-trimmed silk negligee. For an instant, she stared at it, stunned. Then she lifted it from the box. It was extremely sheer. She could see right through it. "A—a night-gown," Cara stuttered. "How pretty."

"For the wedding night," Lila said suggestively.

The other girls whistled and hooted; Cara felt her cheeks flush hot pink. Quickly, she shoved the gown back in the box and reached for another package, hoping her discomfort and embarrassment weren't obvious to her friends.

Of course marriage meant sex. Everybody knew that. So why hadn't it occurred to her? Cara unwrapped a bundle of fluffy yellow bath towels, a gift from Sandy, but her thoughts were about her relationship with Steven. They were very much in love, and they were also great friends. There was nothing Cara liked better than romantic evenings alone with Steven, and the passionate kisses they shared. But they had never slept together. It was Cara's decision. Steven, who was not much older, understood that the time was not right yet for either of them.

As she opened a set of plastic tumblers and an ice bucket from Robin, Cara realized that in all the romantic talk about eloping, she had never actually contemplated the day-to-day realities of married life. Now she tried to picture it: living with Steven, sleeping with Steven. Cara recalled the thought she had had earlier that afternoon. *I actually thought being married wouldn't be all that different from going steady? How stupid could I be?* She could have laughed, except that suddenly she felt very much like crying.

Cara was scared. She did her best to hide her feelings, forcing herself to smile as she unwrapped more sexy lingerie, this time a black lace teddy from Amy. Her heart was pounding, and she wanted nothing more than to run away from this horrible bridal shower. She wished she could turn the clock back, return to the Sunday afternoon when Steven had burst into the apartment and fallen on one knee to propose to her. That afternoon she had not considered the depth of the commitment she was making, and now that she did consider it, she was not at all sure she was ready for it.

As she looked around the room at the faces of her closest friends, Cara felt genuinely torn. Did she really have a choice? Steven's plan seemed to provide the only possible way for her to stay in Sweet Valley. She and Steven wouldn't actually be living *in* Sweet Valley, though; the night before, they had agreed to look for an apartment in San Farando, a town halfway between Sweet Valley and the university. Steven had been willing to do all the commuting, but Cara had insisted on a compromise. It was only fair.

Compromises. How many of them are we going to have to make? Cara shook her head and wished it had never occurred to her that while becoming Steven's wife would solve one problem, it would create countless others.

"What do you want for dinner?" Mrs. Walker called to Cara from the kitchen.

Cara stuck her head out of her room into the hall. "I'm not hungry, actually. I spent the afternoon at Lila's and we really pigged out."

"I think I'll just throw together a salad," Mrs. Walker decided. "You can do the same later, if you want. I picked up a bunch of fresh stuff on my way home from work."

"Sounds good," Cara responded.

The phone rang just as Cara shut her door. She quickly picked up the extension in her bedroom, hoping it was Steven. She needed to hear his voice, to be reminded of how much she loved him.

"Hi, Cara, it's your father," a deep male voice announced.

"Daddy!" A smile of surprise brightened Cara's face. "How are you? What's up?"

"Well, I'll tell you," he said. "Charlie and I have decided to come out and visit you and your mom before you leave for London. We're flying to Sweet Valley for the weekend."

"This weekend?"

"This weekend," Mr. Walker confirmed. "I called your mom at the office today, and she's invited us for dinner tomorrow night."

"That's great, Dad! I can't wait to see you." All of a sudden Cara was overwhelmed by a desire for her father to invite her to go back to Chicago with him and Charlie. She could run away from everything—her mother and London, Steven and marriage, everything.

"I can't wait to see you either, Cara," her father answered. "In fact, I'd fly out even if you weren't going abroad. I have a surprise for you, something I want to tell you about in person."

"A surprise? What is it?" Cara squealed.

Mr. Walker laughed. "It's . . . a surprise. You'll find out tomorrow night."

"Does Mom know what it is?" Cara asked.

"I've talked to your mother about it," Mr. Walker admitted. "Now, that's all I'm saying. See you tomorrow."

"Bye, Dad." Cara replaced the receiver thoughtfully. *Dad has a surprise, something he's talked to Mom about, and something he wants to tell me in person. . . .*

A wild thought popped into Cara's head. Maybe her parents were going to try to get back together! Maybe her father had finally realized he had made a big mistake walking out on his wife and splitting his family in two. And, of course, he saw that if he didn't remedy the situation now, with his ex-wife set to move to England, he might never get another chance.

Dad's coming to Sweet Valley to ask Mom to marry him again! Cara ran down the hall to the kitchen. Mrs. Walker was slicing a red bell pepper for her salad. *How can she just stand there and chop vegetables?* Cara wondered. *She must be so excited!*

"That was Dad," Cara told her mother.

"Really? I talked to him earlier today." Mrs. Walker smiled. "Won't it be fun to see him and Charlie?"

"Yeah, of course." Cara sat on the counter

and looked closely at her mother's face. "So, what's Daddy's secret?"

"I don't precisely know," Mrs. Walker replied, reaching for a bunch of carrots.

"You don't *precisely* know. That means you *do* know, imprecisely," Cara deduced. "You have an idea."

Mrs. Walker laughed at her daughter's logic. "Maybe I have an idea, maybe not. Whatever it is, your father wants to tell you himself."

She handed a carrot to her daughter. Cara munched it and continued to study her mother. Mrs. Walker seemed cheerful, and strangely contented. *She's happy about something*, Cara figured. *It can't be about moving to London; who could be happy about that? It must have something to do with Dad!*

Suddenly, Cara giggled. "What's so funny?" Mrs. Walker asked.

"Oh, nothing." The irony of the situation had just occurred to Cara. She wasn't the only one making secret plans. While she and Steven were talking about getting married, her parents were doing the same thing!

Cara jumped down from the counter and gave her mother an impulsive hug. "I love you, Mom."

Mrs. Walker looked at her daughter in surprise. "I love you, too, honey."

Grabbing another carrot, Cara dashed back to her room. She closed the door and bounced onto her bed. She could not stop smiling. Her mother was acting pretty casually, but Cara could see right through her. It was as clear as glass: her parents had decided to make up.

Cara leaned over the side of the bed and reached under it. She had brought home from Lila's house a few of the smaller gifts she had received; Lila had agreed to keep the larger gifts at her house until after the wedding. Now she pulled out the box containing the negligee from Lila. *I can give this awful thing back,* Cara thought as she fingered the lace. Because if her parents remarried, Mrs. Walker wouldn't have to accept the transfer and move to London. Mr. Walker and Charlie would come back to Sweet Valley for good. They would be a family again, as they used to be, as they should be.

An overwhelming sense of relief washed over Cara. Best of all, if her parents got back together, she and Steven wouldn't have to take drastic measures in order to preserve their relationship. They wouldn't have to get married after all! Cara flopped back against her pillows with a contented sigh. Now, this felt right. *That* was the wedding that would solve all her problems!

Seven

"I have one more place I want to show you," the realtor in San Farando told Steven at five o'clock on Thursday afternoon. "I think it's just what you're looking for."

Steven shrugged. He was running out of steam, but he might as well be thorough. The realtor had taken him to see three other apartments, each of which had struck Steven as too small and too expensive. But he and Cara had to live *somewhere*. "Sure," he said. "I have time to see one more."

He dropped into the passenger seat of the realtor's sporty red convertible. "This one isn't right in town," she mentioned as they turned off San Farando's quaint Main Street onto a side road. "So it's a little less convenient to shopping and transportation. But the rent is lower."

Steven grinned tiredly. "That's a definite plus."

They drove past a few dozen small stucco houses with tiny yards. Finally, the realtor braked in front of an unpretentious apartment building, only a few stories high.

"It's a garden apartment," she informed Steven as they walked around to the back of the building. Steven knew what that meant: ground level, with no view to speak of. The realtor found the correct key on her big key ring and unlocked the door. "Go ahead," she said, waving Steven on in ahead of her. "Get a feel for it."

Steven entered the apartment. It didn't take long to get a feel for the place—there wasn't much to it. He strolled through the three rooms and stuck his head in the closet-sized bathroom.

"What you see is what you get: living room, bedroom, kitchen, bath. Just the basics, but everything's newly renovated. See?" The realtor led him into the kitchen. "Wood cabinets and all new appliances."

Steven dutifully admired the shiny cabinets and sparkling stove and refrigerator. "Not much counter space," he observed, thinking of the spacious, airy kitchen of his family's house in Sweet Valley. "And no room for a dining table, huh?"

"No, there isn't a separate dining area," the realtor agreed. "But you'll be amazed at how much you can do with this large living space."

She waved her hand in the direction of the living room. *Large* was not the adjective Steven would have chosen to describe it.

"There's no getting around it, it's cozy." The realtor gave him a knowing smile. "Just right for newlyweds."

Newlyweds . . . Steven walked over to the windows. The ground-floor apartment looked out over the back lawn, and beyond that a parking lot and some bedraggled palm trees. He turned and faced in again, examining the apartment with a critical eye. He tried to imagine himself and Cara living in the apartment—eating, sleeping, studying. *Where will I put my desk?* Steven wondered. The apartment would certainly ensure togetherness. He and Cara wouldn't be able to get away from each other!

The realtor checked her watch. "So, what do you think?"

"Well . . ." Steven crossed to a closet and opened the door. *Not much room there. Luckily, Cara doesn't have as many clothes as Jessica!* he thought wryly. "What's the rent?"

She named a figure. Steven nodded. It was on the high side of what he and Cara had determined they could afford, but at least it was in their range, unlike the other apartments he had looked at that afternoon. He stood with his hands in his trouser pockets and rocked back on his heels. He knew he should take the apartment. From what he had seen of the market in San Farando, he was probably not going to find anything more suitable or more affordable. *We'll take it.* Just three words, but for some reason, Steven could not bring himself to utter them.

I really shouldn't make a final decision without giving Cara a chance to check out the place first, Steven rationalized. But deep inside, he knew that wasn't what was holding him back. He just wasn't ready. "I like it, and I think she will, too, but I want to talk it over with her before I put any money down. Can I let you know in a couple of days?"

"Sure," the realtor replied. "I'll tell you what. If anyone else is interested, I'll call you and give you first shot at it."

"Thanks. I really appreciate it."

Back in town, Steven shook hands with the realtor and then climbed into his own car. He had intended to look for a part-time job today, as well as an apartment, but now he simply didn't have the energy. He was tired and hungry and discouraged. All he wanted to do was go back to the dorm and hit the sack. *Go to sleep for at least a week,* Steven thought as he sped onto the highway.

Back on campus, Steven parked his car on the far side of the quadrangle, then headed across the lawn. Halfway to the dorm he paused for a moment and took a deep breath of warm, sweet evening air. Rock music wafted from a speaker in a window somewhere and blended with the voices of students playing

Frisbee on the quad. Suddenly, Steven felt as if he were seeing the university for the first time. *What a great place to live*, he thought.

"Heads up, Wakefield!"

Steven whirled in time to field the football that had been tossed at him. Bob, Ted, Eve, and a few other of his friends were staking out a playing field on the lawn. "Want to join us?" Bob invited. "We're organizing a touch football game."

Steven spiraled the ball to Eve. "I kind of blew off the afternoon. I should get inside and study."

"You're no fun anymore," Eve told Steven, punting the ball to Ted.

Steven forced himself to smile. "What can I say? I'm a grind." He waved and continued on toward the dorm, stopping once to look back over his shoulder at Bob and the others. He didn't have time to mess around with his friends now, and with a pang Steven realized that in the future he would *never* have time for that sort of thing. He would still be going to school, but he wouldn't be living on campus. College just wouldn't seem like college anymore.

In the lobby of the dorm, Steven stopped to check his mail. He pulled a sports magazine out of the box, then a letter from a hotel in Nevada, confirming the room he had reserved for the wedding night, Steven guessed. He peered into the mailbox. There was one more letter inside. Steven removed it, then froze when he recognized the official university stationery. *The law program*, he realized, suddenly feeling sick.

For the past few days, Steven had put his application to the program out of his mind. Once he had decided to marry Cara, he didn't want to think about what he would do if he was accepted. He walked upstairs to his room. *There's no point sweating it*, he told himself as he sat down on the couch. *I didn't get in*.

He ripped open the envelope and slid out a folded sheet of paper. Then he opened the letter. The words jumped out at Steven. *Very impressed with your application . . . pleased to inform you . . .* "I'm in," he said out loud.

Steven knew he should be thrilled. He had worked so hard for this. And a week before, he would have been; he would have been shouting the news out the window to his friends, dialing home to share his triumph with his family. Instead, all Steven felt now was trapped. There was no way he could join the law program and still support Cara and himself. The program was intensive; he would barely have time to *see* Cara, much less set up a new life with her. Commuting and the night job would further eat into his study time. No, he couldn't do both. Steven sank back on the couch, his heart heavy. Which was it going to be?

"Steven and Cara are doing *what*?" Todd exclaimed.

Jessica giggled. "Shhh!" Elizabeth said, looking around anxiously. As usual, the Dairi Burger was crowded and noisy. Luckily, it appeared that no one outside of their corner booth had heard Todd.

It was Thursday night. Elizabeth, Jessica, and Sam had met Todd after watching the Sweet Valley High boys' and girls' basketball teams shoot their way to big wins over their Ramsbury High opponents. Elizabeth hadn't intended to tell Todd about Cara and Steven's plans in such a public place, but she had decided she couldn't wait any longer for his opinion.

Sam was astonished, too. "You had something to do with this," he guessed, turning to Jessica. "I knew something was up between you and Steven the other day, when we were watching *Love Story* and all of a sudden you kicked me out of the house."

"Don't tell me this whole thing was your idea," Elizabeth groaned. "I should have known!"

"I only suggested it to Steven," Jessica protested. "*I'm* not the one who popped the question to Cara! I don't know what you're all so upset about, anyway. I think this is great news, and so did all of Cara's friends at the bridal shower today."

"Cara's friends? Bridal shower? I thought this was supposed to be a secret!" Elizabeth exclaimed.

"It wouldn't be any fun to elope if nobody knew about it," Jessica reasoned.

"I assume your *parents* don't know," said Todd, drumming his fingers on the table.

"No. Or Cara's mother, either," Elizabeth retorted.

Sam grinned. "What a wild scheme."

Elizabeth watched Todd, curious to hear what he would suggest they do about the situation. "I always thought Steven had a good head on his shoulders," Todd said at last. "I wouldn't have thought he'd make a mistake like this."

Unexpectedly, Elizabeth found herself jumping to Steven's defense. "He and Cara feel they don't have any choice," she pointed out. "I agree it's a mistake, but it's understandable, don't you think?"

Todd shook his head. "They'll regret tying themselves down so young," he predicted.

"They're not tying themselves down!" Jessica protested. "They're in love."

"But how do they know it's going to last?" Todd challenged.

A silence fell over the group.

"Well, there's still time for them to come to their senses and change their minds," Sam said after a moment.

"They *have* come to their senses," Jessica declared. "And they're not going to change their minds." She turned to Todd. "So don't bother scheming with Liz and trying to foil their plans," she commanded.

"I'm going to stay out of it," Todd assured her.

"Good. Then let's change the subject," Jessica suggested. Todd, Sam, and Jessica began to rehash the basketball teams' victories. Elizabeth only half listened to the conversation. While she had expected Todd to be surprised about Steven and Cara's elopement, she hadn't quite expected him to be so vehemently against it, to take the news quite so personally. He had reacted as if someone were forcing *him* into making a similar decision. Elizabeth contemplated her boyfriend's face. His expression was once again cheerful and animated. Still, Elizabeth wondered why Todd had seemed so threatened by the thought of Steven and Cara's commitment.

As Steven drove in the direction of the Dairi Burger, he was tempted to head back to the university. Cara wasn't expecting him; Mrs. Walker had told him that she had taken a break from studying and gone to the Dairi Burger. But trying to study tonight was futile. He couldn't think of anything but the law program's acceptance letter, now in his jacket pocket. *I don't know why I'm making such a big deal about it*, he thought, turning into the Dairi Burger's parking lot. Then he sighed heavily. Yes, he did know why. Because it *was* a big deal. Whatever he finally decided about the law program would have an impact on the rest of his life. Steven suddenly knew that his instinct to come to Sweet Valley that night was right. He *had* to see Cara; he *had* to talk it over with her. *That's what marriage is all about, right? Making decisions together, sharing responsibilities.*

Steven spotted Cara right away. She was sitting at a booth near the door with Lila, Amy, Amy's boyfriend, Barry Rork, and two other boys. Tennis teammates of Barry's, Steven guessed. For a moment, Steven stood and watched her. All week, Cara had been quiet and contemplative. Steven knew that she, too, had started to think about the seriousness of their decision. Tonight, though, Cara's expression was animated, even carefree. Steven felt a pang of love, sudden and sharp. She was so beautiful. And she was going to be his wife.

As Steven approached the booth, one of the boys said something that made Cara and the others explode into laughter. "Oh, hi, Steven," Cara called, still laughing. "What a surprise!"

He smiled. "Sorry I didn't give you any warning."

"I'd say join us, but we're sitting like sardines as it is," Barry said amiably.

"Hey, no problem." Steven scanned the restaurant to see if there was anyone else there he knew. Just his sisters. The last people he felt like talking to.

"We can probably find a table for two," Cara remarked as she stood up. "See you guys later!"

"I didn't mean to barge in on you and your

friends," Steven said as they looked around for a place to sit.

"That's OK." Cara squeezed his hand. "I'm happy to see you. But there aren't any empty tables after all." Jessica waved at them. Cara waved back. "Those guys have some room. Why don't we—"

"Let's go for a drive," Steven suggested. "To tell you the truth, I'm not really up for a crowd scene."

"OK," Cara agreed. "Where do you want to go? I shouldn't stay out too much longer."

"How about the beach, for a walk by the water?" Steven suggested. "I looked at some apartments this afternoon," he told Cara as they settled into his VW.

"Really?"

"They were pretty nice. I saw one I think you'll like. It's small, but it's in our price range. Maybe we could go look at it together sometime next week."

"Sure."

There was a stretch of silence. Cara wasn't talkative, but she seemed to be in a good mood, humming along to the radio. "What about you?" Steven asked. "How was your day? Did Lila have a party for you?"

"Yeah. It was fun." Cara smiled. "I know why they call them showers. I was showered with presents."

"Any stuff we'll actually be able to use in the new place?"

"Oh, I'll find a use for everything," Cara said breezily.

When they reached the beach, they took each other's hand and set out on the path over the dunes. Ahead of them, the wide, white strip of sand shimmered in the moonlight. Cara stooped to take off her shoes, then ran to the water's edge. Steven came up behind her and put his arms around her. Laughing, Cara twisted to face him. "I'm feeling a little dizzy," she said. "You'd better hold me tight to keep me from falling in!"

"Glad to oblige."

Cara stood on tiptoe to brush his lips with a gentle kiss. "It's all these emotions. I've been up and down like a yo-yo lately."

"Believe me," Steven assured her, "I know how you feel."

"I think I'm heading up for good now!" Cara said as they began to stroll. "My dad called earlier," she added. "He and Charlie are coming to town tomorrow night."

"Really? What's the occasion?"

"Oh, nothing," Cara said. "I think they just want to say goodbye to me and Mom."

"Little do they know you're not going anywhere," Steven said.

"That's right." Cara smiled meaningfully. "Little do they know!"

They reached a big piece of driftwood and sat down, looking out over the limitless expanse of moonlit ocean. Steven put his hand in his pocket and touched the letter. He knew what Cara would say if he told her about his acceptance. She wouldn't let him give up the program. She wouldn't let him make a sacrifice like that.

Steven had considered the situation from every angle. It *was* pretty confusing, but one thing seemed clear: he couldn't marry Cara *and* participate in the law program. Steven put an arm around Cara's slender shoulders. She looked up at him, her dark eyes shining. "Everything's going to work out," she promised him, as if she had read his mind.

At that moment, Steven knew what he had to do. He had no choice but to give up the program. He couldn't let Cara go. It meant it would be a lot harder to realize his dream of becoming a lawyer. After college, he probably wouldn't be able to afford to go to law school full time, but he could always go at night and spread out his legal training over five or six years. He would be a lot older when he finished—if he finished—but at least he would be with Cara. And looking into her loving, smiling eyes, Steven knew that being with Cara was what he wanted more than anything.

They kissed, the warmth of Cara's lips stealing to Steven's heart. "You're right," he murmured. "Everything's going to work out."

Eight

"I thought you'd be spending every possible minute with Cara," Mrs. Wakefield remarked to Steven as the family sat down to dinner on Friday. "Not that it isn't nice to have you here with us!"

"I'll see her tomorrow. Her family's having a sort of reunion tonight," Steven explained. He helped himself to the stir-fried chicken and rice. "Her dad and brother are in town. She was really excited about seeing them."

"I suppose they won't have many opportunities to get together when she and her mother are living in London," Mrs. Wakefield observed.

"Right." Steven met Jessica's eyes across the table. Jessica winked, and Steven frowned at her. Could she be any *less* subtle? It was amazing to him that she had managed to keep the elopement a secret from the family this long.

Not that he was in the clear yet. Jessica still had a week to blow it!

The meal got under way. As usual, each member of the family had news to share. Mr. Wakefield talked about a plan to reorganize his law firm that had been discussed at a partners' meeting that day; Mrs. Wakefield made everyone laugh by describing an odd client for whom she was doing some design work; Elizabeth described her latest reporting assignment for *The Oracle;* Jessica complained about the cost of the new cheerleading uniforms, the fact that Robin had picked them out, and that they were boring. Only Steven was quiet. He felt strangely apart, as if he were already an outsider. *It'll never be the same once I'm married,* he realized sadly. His home would be with Cara. She would be his family. He would be a guest at his parents' house, no longer just one of the kids.

But that was the way life worked, Steven told himself. It happened sooner or later; in his case, it was going to be sooner, that was all. Because he had made up his mind. He was still carrying the law program's letter in his jacket pocket. He had read and reread it a dozen times and he knew he was making an enormous sacrifice, but his decision to decline the offer was firm. And he had made another resolution: not to tell anyone, including his family and Cara, that he had been accepted. Cara would only feel guilty if she knew, and he couldn't tell his parents why he was turning down the program without revealing his wedding plans. As for Elizabeth . . . Steven knew she would never understand why he was turning his back on the chance to realize his dream. She would try to talk him out of it; they would just have another fight.

Steven set down his fork. He might as well get this over with. He cleared his throat. "Um, I have something to tell everybody."

Jessica stared at Steven, her eyes round. *She probably thinks I'm about to come clean about the secret wedding!* Steven thought ironically. "I heard from the law program. My application was turned down."

"Oh, Steven." Mrs. Wakefield's forehead creased in a frown. "I'm sorry." She took her son's hand and squeezed it.

Steven squeezed back. "Me, too, Mom."

"You gave it your best shot," Mr. Wakefield said supportively. "You should be proud of that."

Steven nodded. He didn't trust himself to speak.

"It may take a little longer, but you'll still be a lawyer someday," Mrs. Wakefield told him. "We believe in you."

"That's right." Mr. Wakefield grinned. "You and I will be partners yet!"

"I hope so, Dad," Steven said.

Steven looked across the table at his sisters. Jessica looked relieved. She had probably guessed that the law program would put a strain on his married life with Cara. Elizabeth, however, had frozen, her fork lifted halfway to her mouth. Reluctantly, Steven met Elizabeth's eyes and read the question there. He only hoped she couldn't read the lie in his own eyes.

"Mmm, that dip is good," Cara said, sampling it with a carrot stick.

"It was always your dad's favorite," Mrs. Walker remarked.

Cara couldn't help but smile as she watched her mother arrange cheese and crackers on a tray. She was making her ex-husband's favorite dinner. It could mean only one thing!

Mom is really sly, Cara thought as she sliced fresh vegetables for the dip. As the moment of her father's arrival neared, Cara felt more and more convinced that her parents were going to try to get back together again. Mrs. Walker was probably just going through the motions as she continued to make arrangements for the move to London. The moving plans would come to a halt as soon as her parents' reconciliation became official.

Cara carried the hors d'oeuvres into the living room. She had just finished plumping up the pillows on the couch when the doorbell rang. "Hi, Daddy!" she called into the intercom. "Hi, Charlie. I'll buzz you up!"

Cara raced to the door when she heard footsteps in the hall. She flung the door open, ready to smother her father with a giant bear hug. Instead, she froze. Mr. Walker and Charlie weren't alone. An unfamiliar, auburn-haired woman was standing with them.

Charlie jumped on Cara and squeezed her with all his might. "I've missed you!"

"Me, too," Cara said, her voice flat and distracted. She could not take her eyes off the woman, who, to Cara's annoyance, was smiling at her in a fond, familiar way. "Uh, hi, Dad."

"Hi, Cara. Is it ever good to see you!" Mr. Walker stooped to plant a kiss on his daughter's forehead. "You look wonderful. So do you, Jacqueline!"

Cara turned to see that her mother had come up behind her. Now Mrs. Walker smiled as her ex-husband took both her hands in his and kissed her lightly on the cheek. Then she wrapped her arms tightly around her son. Meanwhile, Mr. Walker stepped back and put a hand under the other woman's elbow in order to bring her forward. "Cara and Jacqueline, this is my friend Julia."

His friend Julia? Stunned, Cara looked from Mr. Walker to Julia to Mrs. Walker. *Why doesn't Mom look shocked?* she wondered.

"It's very nice to meet you," Mrs. Walker said, smiling graciously and extending her hand.

"And you," Julia replied warmly.

"Come in, all of you!" Mrs. Walker urged.

Cara followed her family and Julia into the

living room. Her father and his "friend" sat down side by side on the couch. *Mom's supposed to be sitting there with him*, Cara thought. *What's going on?* As Mrs. Walker poured glasses of fresh lemonade for everyone, Mr. Walker edged closer to Julia on the sofa. Cara watched in horror as her father took Julia's hand in his.

"I don't see any reason to put off telling you the news." Mr. Walker smiled at Cara. "I think your mother may already know what I'm going to say." Cara looked at her mother. Mrs. Walker was smiling, too, although Cara thought she could detect a trace of uncertainty in the fine lines around her mouth. Mr. Walker beamed at Julia, and then at his daughter. "Julia and I are going to be married."

"Why, that's wonderful," Mrs. Walker exclaimed. "I should be serving champagne instead of lemonade!"

Cara sank back in her chair as if she had been shot. The shock had taken her breath away. Both her father and Julia looked at her hopefully, expectantly. Cara knew she was supposed to say something. But what? She couldn't express what she was actually feeling, that this was the most horrible news she had ever heard, the worst news since her parents had announced they were getting a divorce.

In the picture of her father's new life with his fiancée, Cara saw the disintegration of her final hope. The irony was too cruel. Her father was getting married, all right—but to the wrong woman! *Can Dad possibly expect me to be happy for him, happy about the fact that he's ruined my life?* Cara wondered. "Congratulations," she said finally, her voice devoid of all emotion.

"Unfortunately, this is going to be a short visit. There won't be nearly enough time for you and Julia to get to know each other," Mr. Walker told Cara. "But I hope you know we'll always have a room for you at our new home. And we want you to visit as often as you can!"

"Not that you'll want to leave London! You're going to love it," Julia predicted. "I lived there for a few years, and when the time came for me to return to the United States, I didn't *want* to come back."

Then why did you? Cara thought angrily.

"Oh, we'd love to talk to you about London!" Mrs. Walker declared. "You can give us some tips about what to do and see while we get oriented."

"I'd be happy to," Julia said.

Is Mom serious? Cara thought. *Daddy just replaces her with another woman and Mom wants to chat with her about sightseeing?*

And what about Charlie? Cara looked at her little brother. He had to be upset about this, too. He couldn't want a stranger intruding into his home, trying to replace his mother. But Charlie looked far from upset. He seemed comfortable around Julia; he actually seemed to *like* her.

Charlie intercepted Cara's distraught, questioning gaze. "You have to come to Chicago sometime," he said, as if he was trying to make his sister feel included in the new family that was taking shape. "We'll go to a baseball game. Julia's a nut about the Cubs."

"That's right." Julia laughed. "I grew up a few blocks from Wrigley Field. I guess it's in the blood."

A timer went off in the kitchen. Mrs. Walker rose to her feet. "Can I help you?" Julia asked.

"No, thanks." Mrs. Walker caught her daughter's eye. "Cara can give me a hand."

Cara followed her mother into the kitchen. As soon as they were alone, Cara put her hands on her hips, her dark eyes accusing. "Did you know about this?"

Mrs. Walker opened the oven to check on the game hens stuffed with wild rice. "I suspected something of the sort when your father told me he was bringing Julia."

"He told you she was coming?"

"Well, he couldn't exactly have just shown up at the door with her!" Mrs. Walker removed the fresh asparagus from the refrigerator. "It was only polite to let me know in advance. Besides, I think he wanted me to have time to get used to the idea of him being with another woman."

"Well, what about me?" Cara demanded. "Didn't it occur to him that *I* might need time to get used to the idea?"

Mrs. Walker was startled by her daughter's

vehemence. "I guess it didn't," she said. "Cara, I know this is sudden, but give Julia a chance—"

"Don't tell me what to do." Cara's voice shook with barely suppressed anger. Trying to maintain her self-control, Cara turned her back on her mother, and quickly left the kitchen.

For Cara, the meal was a nightmare. Everybody else seemed genuinely happy about Mr. Walker's announcement. Julia had obviously spent a lot of time with Charlie; the two laughed at private jokes and prompted each other to tell stories about life in Chicago. Even Mrs. Walker seemed to take to Julia. She plied Julia with questions about London, which Julia was only too happy to answer. Then there was Cara's father and the way he just seemed to sit back and enjoy the bizarre spectacle of his former and future wives merrily chatting. In Cara's opinion, it was absolutely revolting.

Cara could hardly bring herself to say a word, in spite of Julia's good-natured attempts to draw her out. "Tell me what you're looking forward to most," Julia asked Cara. "London has a wonderful theater district, and the architecture is magnificent. Is history your thing? Or shopping? I bet it's shopping!"

"I don't like shopping," Cara said quietly.

Mr. Walker chuckled. "Then you've *really* changed. What happened to the Cara who used to spend all day at the mall with Jessica and Lila?"

She's gone, Cara answered silently. She shrugged and said nothing.

Julia wasn't discouraged. She continued to talk up the attractions of London. By dessert, Cara felt that if she heard one more word about how wonderful London was and how lucky she was to be moving there, she would scream. When Mrs. Walker rose to pour the coffee, Cara stood up as well. "Excuse me," she mumbled, "but I have to make a phone call."

She hurried from the room. As soon as she was out of sight of her family and Julia, the tears began to flow. In her room, Cara shut and locked the door, then threw herself face down on the bed and sobbed. The emotional roller coaster she had been riding had taken a downward turn. Cara felt herself heading for a crash.

Saying that she had a headache, Cara managed to avoid talking any more to her father and Julia that evening. As she lay alone on her bed staring at the ceiling, her profound sense of betrayal grew. Things were supposed to be different. Her parents were supposed to reconcile so that they could be a family again in Sweet Valley. So that Cara didn't have to get married.

Instead, her parents had let her down. Again.

Cara listened to the muffled sounds of voices as her mother said good night to Mr. Walker and Julia, who were staying in a hotel in town for the weekend. Then she heard Charlie running water in the bathroom. When she heard him settle down on the pull-out couch, Cara left her room.

She found her mother in the kitchen. For a moment she wasn't sure exactly what she wanted to say to her, but then all the hurt and disappointment she felt came rushing to the surface, and with the emotions came words. "How could you just stand there and do nothing about all of this, Mom?"

Mrs. Walker's dark eyebrows lifted. "Cara, what do you mean?"

"How can you be so happy that your husband is marrying someone else?"

A flicker of pain crossed Mrs. Walker's face. "Cara, I know this isn't easy for you. It's not easy for me, either, but—"

Cara shook her head. "You didn't even try!" she whispered, hoping not to wake Charlie. "We had a chance to be a family again, and you didn't even *try*."

"That's not fair, Cara, and you know it," Mrs. Walker said.

"Well, you can screw up your own life if you want, but I'm not going to let you screw up mine!" Cara declared. She turned and stormed back to her bedroom.

She had meant what she said. She wasn't sad or scared anymore; she was mad. Her parents didn't care about her feelings. They didn't care that the decisions they made about their own lives were ruining *her* life. Well, she didn't need them anymore. She didn't want to live with her mother in London; she didn't want to visit her father and Julia in Chicago. That left only one option: Steven. Cara's determination grew. She would show her parents that she wasn't their pawn, that she was in charge of her own life. She would start a family of her own. She would marry Steven after all.

Nine

"Hi!" Jessica said to her brother on Wednesday afternoon. "What are you doing here?" Steven glanced around, as if to determine whether anyone else was there to overhear. "Don't worry. Mom and Dad aren't home yet and Liz is outside by the pool with Todd."

Jessica had just selected a bunch of green grapes from the refrigerator for that day's post-cheerleading-practice snack. Steven grabbed one of the grapes and popped it in his mouth. "I just had my blood test. Now I have to go to the jewelry store. The rings are ready."

"You've certainly put enough mileage on your car in the past couple of weeks," Jessica observed.

"Tell me about it," Steven replied.

Jessica settled into a chair at the table and

flipped open the latest issue of her favorite fashion magazine. "Is Cara going with you?"

"No. I want her ring to be sort of a surprise. You know, because of the engraving. I want her to see it for the first time on Saturday."

"Saturday." Jessica grinned. "Can you believe it? The big day is only three days away!" Steven pretended to chew on his fingernails. Jessica giggled. "Well, since Cara's not going, can I come with you?"

"Sure. I'd like the company. I just have to run upstairs. The receipt from the jeweler is in my desk."

A few minutes later, the two walked out to Steven's car. "There's nothing wrong with Cara, is there?" Jessica asked her brother. "She didn't show up for practice again today."

Steven shrugged. "She's been having a lot of headaches lately. I think seeing her dad and brother this past weekend was harder than she expected, especially with Mr. Walker bringing along his new girlfriend. I mean, it's natural that she should be sort of . . . emotional."

"*You're* not getting cold feet, are you?" Jessica teased.

She thought Steven would laugh, but instead his expression remained serious. "No," he said after a pause. "My feet are OK. Firmly on the ground."

"Well, that's good," Jessica said lightly.

Steven opened the driver's-side door of the

VW. "Oops. I think I left the car keys on my desk," he said as he patted his pocket. "I'm getting very forgetful!"

"I'll run up," Jessica offered.

She trotted inside and up the stairs to Steven's room. As he had predicted, the VW keys were on his desk. Jessica grabbed them and turned to leave. As she did she spotted an envelope lying on the floor. She picked it up and examined the return address curiously. *The letter from the law program. He must have dropped it,* Jessica observed. *Poor Steven, carrying the letter around with him. It must have been really painful for him, being turned down by the program he had wanted to get into so badly.* Without even thinking about her action, Jessica slipped the letter from the envelope and unfolded it. Once she had gone that far, there didn't seem to be anything wrong with actually reading the letter. After all, it wasn't as if the contents were a secret. She already *knew* what it said.

Or did she? Jessica's eyes widened as she read. Instead of the apologetic "We regret to inform you" type of phrases she had expected, the letter contained glowing praise of Steven's exceptional academic record. "He got in," Jessica exclaimed. "He told us he didn't, but he *did*!"

Jessica put the letter back in the envelope. She dropped it on the floor, then nudged it with her toe until it was partly under the desk. That way no one else would notice it and when

Steven found it again, he wouldn't suspect that anyone had read it. She hurried downstairs to rejoin her brother, her head spinning. Hard as it was to believe, Steven, one of the most honest people Jessica knew, had lied about being rejected by the law program. The big question was, *why?*

With an irritated gesture, Elizabeth shoved her slipping sunglasses back up onto the bridge of her nose. Then she sighed. She was trying to study, but it was no use. She couldn't concentrate.

She dropped her history book onto the white pavement of the poolside patio. The sound caused Todd to look up from his own book. "What's the matter, Liz?" he asked.

"I can't think about anything but Steven and Cara," she confessed. "I'm just so worried about them. Todd, I really think they're going to go through with it."

"I know. Three days from now . . ."

Elizabeth pressed her hands to her ears. "Don't remind me! I don't want to think about it."

"But you *are* thinking about it." Todd smiled wryly. "That's the problem, right?"

"It's because I care about Steven," Elizabeth said. "I mean, he's my brother. I love him. I want the best for him, and this marriage . . . it's not the best. I just can't stand to see him making such a terrible mistake. Todd, we have to try to stop them."

Todd shook his head. "I think it's a mistake, too. But there's nothing we can do about it. You told Steven how you felt, right?"

Elizabeth recalled the brief conversation she had had with Steven in his dorm room. "Sort of. He wouldn't listen to me!"

"That's his prerogative," Todd pointed out. "Liz, he's an adult. He has the right to make his own decisions. If you love him, you have to trust him. You told him your opinion. He knows you're concerned. You've done all you can do."

Elizabeth was glad she was wearing sunglasses; for some reason, she didn't want Todd to see the tears in her eyes. Maybe Todd was right, but his words hadn't made her feel any better. "It's just not the way it should be," Elizabeth said softly. "Steven's wedding day should be something his whole family knows about— and is happy about. We should all be there with him."

"Maybe you'll get another chance," Todd suggested. "If this marriage doesn't work out, and odds are it won't, Steven will probably get married again someday."

"Todd!" Elizabeth cried. "How can you say that?"

"Well, it's true, isn't it?"

Elizabeth couldn't disagree. Still, it was the last thing she wanted to hear. "It just sounds so . . . cold. So cynical."

"I'm sorry." Elizabeth heard a strange note in Todd's voice—a sad, sharp edge. "But that's the way all this makes me feel."

Around front, a car door slammed. Before Elizabeth could respond to Todd's remark, Jessica raced around the side of the house. "Where've you been?" Elizabeth asked, pushing her glasses up on top of her head.

"I went on an errand with Steven. He just dropped me off," Jessica explained. She flopped into a chair next to her sister. "I'm glad you're both here. I have to tell you about something really strange!" Quickly, she told Elizabeth and Todd about reading the letter from the law program. "Don't you think it's weird that Steven lied to us about it? Why would he do that?"

To Elizabeth, Steven's motives were only too obvious. Distressed, she glanced at Todd; she could see that he had figured it out, too. "Don't you see?" Elizabeth asked Jessica. "Steven knows he can't join the law program *and* marry Cara, so he's making us think he was rejected. He's giving up his future for her."

Jessica frowned. "But he *dreamed* of getting into that program. It's all he's talked about for the past few months! Now he's just going to give it up?"

"It looks that way." Elizabeth stared hard at Jessica. "Do you still think it's incredibly romantic that Steven and Cara are getting married?"

Jessica's expression became uncharacteristically

solemn. "I never thought about what was going to happen *after* the wedding," she admitted. "I just figured they'd live happily ever after."

"It's not that easy," Elizabeth said. "And it's what happens after that really matters. Marriage doesn't end with the wedding; that's where it *starts*."

Jessica seemed to be digesting this information. "Things are really going to change for Steven and Cara after they get married, aren't they?" she said finally.

Elizabeth nodded. "Steven's not the only one who'll be making sacrifices. Cara's going to have to adjust, too. It's not going to be like a movie, Jess. This is real life."

Jessica slouched in her chair. "You know," she said thoughtfully, "whenever I thought about Cara and Steven's elopement, I pictured them driving off into the sunset with Just Married streamers billowing from their car." She paused and sighed. "But now . . . I mean, I never imagined that Steven would have to give up the law program, or neglect his school work because he has to pump gas or something, and Cara quitting the cheerleading squad and never having the time or money to go shopping . . ." Jessica shuddered. "Husband and wife. What a drag! You know," she said to Elizabeth and Todd, "Cara and Steven are already almost as boring as you two."

"Gee, thanks," Elizabeth said dryly. Todd's eyebrows pulled together in a frown.

"If they get married," Jessica continued, "they'll be no fun at all! Maybe it *wouldn't* be so bad if Cara moved to London. I could visit her over the summer!"

"Well, it's too late for that," Elizabeth snapped. "Thanks to your great advice, Steven and Cara are eloping."

Maybe it's not too late, Jessica thought. It wouldn't be too late until the moment when Cara and Steven exchanged rings at the chapel in Nevada and said "I do," and that was still three days away. A lot could happen in three days. "Liz, you're supposed to babysit for the Millers tonight, aren't you?"

"Don't remind me!" Elizabeth groaned. "Those kids are such brats!"

"Let me take the job for you," Jessica pleaded.

"You *hate* babysitting and you want to baby-sit for the Millers?" Elizabeth asked.

"Yep!" Jessica confirmed.

"Well, OK." Elizabeth narrowed her eyes. "But I know you're up to something," she said.

Jessica smiled but said nothing. She, who had worked so hard to help arrange the upcoming wedding, had decided to try to stop Steven and Cara from making the biggest mistake of their lives.

*   *   *

"You got a job? Steven, that's great! Is it at the law firm you were telling me about?"

Steven had called Cara from a pay phone, having stopped in San Farando on his way back to the university from Sweet Valley. "No." Cara heard the disappointment in his voice. "They didn't have any part-time paralegal positions. Even if they had, they said they hired only college graduates. Anyway, I have classes three afternoons a week. I need something at night."

"So what did you get?"

"I'm going to be a waiter at Pedro's!"

"A waiter at Pedro's?" Pedro's was the small Mexican restaurant in San Farando where the Wakefields occasionally met Steven for dinner.

He laughed. "Let me tell you about the specials. Would you like to see a wine list?" he joked.

Cara bit her lip. She didn't think it was funny. *Steven's supposed to be a lawyer, not a waiter*. "Steven, you don't need to work. I'll—I'll get a job," Cara offered, even though she had no idea of what kind of job she might like or be qualified for.

"No way," Steven said firmly. "You spend a lot more hours in school every week than I do. My schedule is much more flexible. Hey, it's going to be fun! I get to wear black trousers and a black vest—I'll look pretty sharp."

She smiled. "I bet you will."

"And I think the tips will be pretty good,"

Steven predicted. "Pedro's is always packed. I mean, I won't make a mint but it should be enough for us to scrape by on. I stopped in at the realtor's, too," he continued. "We have an appointment to look at the apartment on Friday afternoon. Can you meet me here then?"

"Of course. I can't wait to see the place," she lied.

"You'll like it," he assured her, his heartiness sounding somewhat forced to Cara. "I'll talk to you later. I love you."

"I love you, too. Bye." Cara hung up the phone and flopped back on her bed. *Enough to scrape by* . . . She hadn't thought about what it would be like not to have very much money. Two people living on one part-time income. She and Steven would really have to stick to a strict budget.

The phone rang again. With a groan, Cara grabbed the receiver. "Hello," she said in a cranky voice.

"Cara, it's Jessica."

"Jess, what's up?"

"I have a big favor to ask you," Jessica replied. "I'm supposed to be Lila's partner in a doubles tournament at the country club tonight and I completely forgot that I'd promised to babysit for the Millers down the street. I can't leave them without a sitter at the last minute. Will you take the job for me?"

"Jess, I'm really not in the mood—"

"Please, Cara," Jessica begged. "You're my

last hope. Liz and Amy are both busy. It won't be so bad. They only have three kids."

"*Only* three kids?" Cara laughed. "That sounds like three too many to me."

"Come on, Cara," Jessica wheedled. "You'll make a few extra bucks and besides, it will be good experience."

"Good experience?"

"Sure," Jessica said. "You and Steven will probably have tons of kids. You may as well start to learn something about them!"

"Whoa!" Cara exclaimed, startled by Jessica's line of reasoning. "First of all, I very much doubt we'll have *tons* of kids, and second of all, we're not going to have any for an extremely long time."

"You can't be sure of that," Jessica pointed out. "You know the facts of life as well as I do. Even when you use birth control, accidents can happen."

Cara quickly put thoughts of children—wanted or unwanted—out of her mind. But after barely surviving the rest of her father's visit the previous weekend, Cara had been going to great lengths to avoid her mother. "OK, I'll babysit for you."

"Thanks a million," Jessica said.

Cara regretted her generosity as soon as Mr. and Mrs. Miller headed off to a dinner party, leaving her alone with their three children, five-year-old Mark, three-year-old Kathy, and baby Pamela. It seemed to Cara as if Pamela cried for four hours straight: sometimes her diaper needed changing, sometimes she wanted her bottle, and sometimes she seemed to be crying for no other reason than to let off steam. And as if Pamela weren't enough of a handful, Mark and Kathy required constant supervision. Mark tried to give Kathy a haircut with scissors he had found in his mother's sewing basket, and Kathy tried to copy the floral pattern of the dining room wallpaper on the floor with crayons. When their bedtime finally rolled around, Cara thought she might finally have some peace. But as soon as she shut Mark's bedroom door, she heard Kathy's bang open. While she was wrestling Kathy back into bed, Mark made a break for the kitchen for a snack.

Finally, the children fell asleep from sheer exhaustion. Cara checked on the baby, then collapsed on the den couch, ready to pass out herself. She felt as if she had just run a marathon. *Is this what it's like to have kids?* she wondered, too tired to be horrified. If so, she *definitely* wasn't ready to have any of her own. Maybe in another decade . . . or two. She and Steven would have to be careful, that was for sure. But as Jessica said, accidents can happen. . . .

Using the remote control, Cara turned on the TV, hoping to lose herself in a good movie. As she flipped from station to station she saw a baby food commercial, followed by an ad for toilet bowl cleanser and then one for frozen dinners sure to satisfy a hungry man's appetite.

Cara turned down the volume and squeezed her eyes shut. Now, instead of the TV, Cara heard Steven's voice when he had called to tell her about the job at Pedro's. She hated thinking of him waiting tables. He would never have taken the job if it weren't for the fact that they were getting married. If it weren't for her, he would continue to spend his evenings in the library, studying.

His grades will probably suffer, Cara imagined. *And what about my grades?* She hadn't really thought about it before, but it occurred to her now that marriage was going to be a pretty big distraction. She was a competent student, but good grades did not come easily for her. How would she manage to keep up with her homework? Cara remembered how close Jessica had recently come to failing math. What if that happened to her? What if she failed a class or two? What if she didn't graduate?

Unlike Steven, Cara didn't have a firm sense of what she wanted to do with the rest of her life. She had always figured that she had plenty of time to decide on a career—the rest of high school and four years of college, in fact. But what if she never even made it to college? Cara opened her eyes and stared dully at the silent images on the TV screen. What kind of future would she have then? *I'll have Steven*, Cara reminded herself. Still, she had an uneasy feeling that being with Steven might not be enough to make up for the disappointment of other lost opportunities.

Sighing, Cara flipped to a sitcom and turned the volume back up. She loved Steven with all her heart, but she was starting to see that marriage involved a lot more than she had bargained for. Sex, parenthood, financial hardship, less fun, less freedom. What were she and Steven getting themselves into?

Ten

As far as Jessica could tell, phase one of her plot to reveal the unpleasant side of married life to Cara had been a success. At lunch in the cafeteria on Thursday, Cara told horror stories about her night with the Miller children. To Jessica's dismay, however, Cara ended up laughing off the incident, and gave no indication that she was reconsidering her decision to elope with Steven. *I've got to keep working on her*, Jessica determined.

When the final bell rang, Jessica caught up with Cara at her locker. "No practice today," she announced. "How about a trip to the mall?"

Cara greeted the suggestion with enthusiasm. "I would *love* a trip to the mall. I need a little shopping therapy, and an ice cream cone from Casey's wouldn't hurt, either. I'm starting to get a little jittery," she confided.

They headed to the student parking lot together. "I'm not surprised," Jessica commented. "You must be *terrified*."

"Well, that's kind of a strong word," Cara said. "Just nervous, that's all." She looked anxiously at Jessica. "That's natural, isn't it?"

"Of course," Jessica assured her. "Any woman in her right mind would be. After all, it's still a man's world. Women are still oppressed by the institution of marriage." Jessica had quickly studied up on the latest statistics, and she had no qualms about embellishing them a little in order to paint the worst possible picture of married life. "Even though most women today have careers, they still do almost ninety percent of the housework and about ninety-nine percent of the child care. It's like having three jobs, except that you only get paid for one!"

Cara looked startled. "It won't be that way with Steven and me. I'm sure that someday, when we have careers and a family and all that, we'll *both* take care of the housework and raising the kids. We'll be equals."

As they climbed into the Fiat, Jessica glanced quickly at her friend. Cara didn't look half as confident as she sounded. "I just wouldn't take it for granted, that's all." Jessica started the engine. "Sometimes the most liberal, sensitive guys turn out to be pretty old-fashioned at heart."

Cara was silent on the drive to the mall. When they arrived, Jessica wouldn't let Cara even peek into any of their favorite clothing boutiques. Instead, she hustled her to the bed-and-bath section of Lytton and Brown's department store. "So, what color sheets and towels are you thinking about buying for the new apartment?" Jessica asked briskly.

"Sheets and towels? We haven't exactly talked about—"

"Look at this." Jessica pulled Cara to a sale display. "A shower curtain and matching bath mat. It's a good price, too."

"Jessica, I'm not really interested in bath mats," Cara said. "Can't we—"

"Sure. Let's look at the housewares!"

In the housewares department, Jessica dragged Cara from vacuum cleaners to food processors to frying pans, happily noting that Cara appeared more bored and discouraged with every appliance. From housewares they moved on to the book department, where Jessica rapidly collected a dozen horribly tacky titles including *Do-It-Yourself Plumbing* and *Microwave Meals for Two on a Budget.* She piled the books into Cara's arms. "Cooking for Steven is going to be a pain, with all the food allergies he has," Jessica exaggerated.

Cara looked worried. "But I hate cooking."

"Well, *Steven's* not going to have time to cook, with classes and homework and a part-time job," Jessica pointed out. "You have to eat, don't you?"

"Maybe we can just order pizza," Cara suggested.

"It's not very economical," Jessica said in a righteous tone.

Cara shoved the books back at her friend. "Jessica, I don't want to think about these things right now, OK?"

"OK," Jessica agreed. But when Cara began to drift toward the books on travel, Jessica grabbed her arm and yanked her away. "You must be kidding," she exclaimed. "You think you guys are going to have the money to travel? You'll be lucky if you can pay the rent from one month to the next!"

Cara frowned. "We're not going to be *that* poor. At least, I don't think we are. Come on, let's go."

As they were about to leave the book department Jessica paused to examine the titles on the "Hobbies" shelf. "No, you can't take up gardening since you're going to live in a tiny apartment with no yard. Knitting maybe?"

Cara stopped next to Jessica. "Why do I need to take up *anything*?"

"You're going to be spending a lot of time alone over the next year or so," Jessica explained. "I mean, I suppose you could just waste your time watching TV at night while Steven's working at Pedro's."

"Can't I just hang around with you and Amy and Lila and everybody the way I do now?"

Jessica shook her head sadly. "Cara, you're getting *married*. Things'll be different. For one thing, you're going to live in another town. And you'll have tons of new responsibilities. You won't be a kid anymore."

"Just because I'm getting married doesn't mean I have to give up my friends. I'll still be the same person," Cara insisted.

"Maybe not," Jessica replied. "Aren't you going to take Steven's name? Aren't you going to be Mrs. Steven Wakefield?"

Cara's jaw dropped. "I—we haven't discussed it."

"Well, that probably means Steven assumes you'll take his name," said Jessica, although she imagined her brother would want Cara to do whatever she wanted to do.

When they left Lytton and Brown's, they walked slowly to Casey's Place. Jessica could see that Cara was pensive. *She's weakening. I'll give her one more little push.* Ice cream cones in hand, they sat down at a table in Casey's. "You know, we're really going to miss you," Jessica told Cara.

"What do you mean?" Cara asked. "I'm staying right here! That's the whole point, right?"

"In some ways, though, you might as well be moving to London," Jessica said. "You and Steven are taking a really big step. You'll be leaving the rest of us *far* behind."

*   *   *

Steven signed his name to the lease below Cara's and returned the clipboard to the realtor, along with a check for the first month's rent plus security deposit.

The realtor beamed at Steven and Cara. "It's all yours." She handed Steven a set of keys. "If you have any problems around the place, the building manager, Mrs. Redman in unit four, should be able to help you."

"Thanks for everything," Steven said. Cara smiled weakly.

"I'm glad I was able to help. Enjoy your new home!"

The realtor left. Cara and Steven stood in the empty apartment, looking everywhere but at each other. Steven jingled the keys; Cara bit her lip. *Steven was right*, she thought. The apartment *was* small. And there were hardly any windows. "I think it could be a cute place," she said, turning away from Steven and hoping he couldn't sense her uncertainty.

"Definitely," he agreed. "Hey, any apartment would look kind of bare with no furniture. Wait until we get it fixed up."

He came up behind her and put his arms around her, resting his chin on top of her head. Steven's embrace usually made Cara feel secure. But today, she felt something different. She felt trapped.

Gently, Cara detached herself from Steven, pretending that she wanted to look out one of the windows. A little stretch of lawn, a parking lot. Cara couldn't help but compare the restricted view to the view from her bedroom window in Sweet Valley—and the view from the room that would be hers in London if she moved with her mother. *But I'm not moving with Mom*, Cara reminded herself. *Like the realtor said, this is my home now.*

Suddenly, it all seemed terribly real. Too real. At the same time the next day, she and Steven would be checking into their hotel in Nevada. Cara would be a married woman. *Mrs. Steven Wakefield*. Cara shivered.

"What's the matter?" Steven asked her. "What are you thinking about?"

Facing him, she forced herself to smile. "I was just thinking about a conversation Jessica and I had yesterday. We were talking about whether or not I should change my name when I get married. You know, to Cara Wakefield instead of Cara Walker."

"We won't be any less married if you keep your own name," said Steven.

"That's true." The name *didn't* really matter, Cara realized. No matter what she decided about her name, she was going to change as a person. *I won't be the old Cara Walker anymore, no matter what. She'll be gone forever.* Suddenly Cara understood her situation in a new way. Getting married wasn't the problem. A marriage could be anything two people wanted to make it. It could be wonderful. But what if the two people hadn't finished making *themselves*?

Scared, Cara turned to Steven, hoping the feel of his arms around her would dispel her fears and make everything all right. But once again, his embrace seemed somehow smothering. Cara pressed her face against Steven's broad chest and squeezed her eyes shut against the sight of the apartment's four walls. She had been thinking of marriage to Steven as an escape. She didn't want to see what she was seeing now: that it might also be a dead end, for both of them.

Cara was sitting on her bed in the dark on Friday evening, a cool breeze from the open window ruffling her long brown hair, when someone knocked on her bedroom door. "Hey, Cara, it's me."

Cara recognized Jessica's voice. She switched on a light and crossed the room to open the door. "Hi! What are you doing here?"

Jessica stepped into the bedroom and Cara closed the door again. "Your mom let me in," Jessica explained in a low voice. "I just wanted to say goodbye."

"It's not really goodbye," Cara said lightly. "I'll be back on Sunday!"

"I know." There was a serious, almost sad, expression in Jessica's usually bright eyes. "But it's still goodbye. I'm never going to visit you here again. I'm never going to visit you as just my old friend Cara. Next time I see you, you'll be a married woman."

Cara dropped her eyes from Jessica's and resisted the urge to cry. *But I want to stay your old friend Cara. I don't want to be a married woman!*

"I can't stay long," Jessica told Cara. "Sam's waiting outside in the car. We're on our way to a party at Ken's."

"Really?" Cara said wistfully. A party at Ken Matthews's house was nothing special; she had been to dozens of them over the years. But for some reason, that night there was nothing Cara would have liked more than to hang out with her friends.

I'm getting married tomorrow, Cara reminded herself. *This isn't an ordinary Friday night. I'm not a kid anymore. I don't belong with the others.*

"I have something for you," Jessica continued. "To wear during the ceremony tomorrow. You know, something borrowed, something blue and all that."

Cara laughed. "I'd forgotten about that tradition."

Jessica reached into her shoulder bag and handed Cara a pale blue hair ribbon. "That's something new *and* something blue." She smiled. "Two in one."

Cara ran a finger along the glossy satin ribbon. "It's beautiful. You were really sweet to think of this."

"Well, that's not all." Putting her hands to her neck, Jessica unclasped the gold lavaliere she always wore. The necklace had been a sixteenth-birthday present from Jessica's parents. Elizabeth wore an identical one. "I thought you might want to wear this, now that you're going to be my sister. Of course, it's something old *and* borrowed. I want it back!"

Cara was deeply touched. Tears sprang to her eyes as Jessica fastened the necklace around her neck. "Thanks, Jess," Cara whispered. "There's nobody I'd rather have for a sister than you."

"It's a pretty good fringe benefit of your marrying my brother," Jessica agreed. "That reminds me, I almost forgot to tell you! You really should know this. I found a letter in Steven's room the other day, a letter from that law program at the university. It wasn't even close to being a rejection letter! They were practically begging him to join the program!"

"You mean, he was *accepted* by the law program after all?" Cara asked.

"That's right," Jessica confirmed. "I guess he decided to turn down the offer and he didn't want any of us to know. He must have figured he couldn't focus exclusively on academics if he was married. That really proves it, doesn't it? He must *really* love you to give up something that important for you."

Cara could only nod. All at once, she felt terribly guilty. If what Jessica said was true, Steven

119

was willing to sacrifice his entire future for her. That put an awful lot of responsibility on Cara's shoulders, and she wasn't sure she wanted that burden.

Cara looked up to catch Jessica watching her speculatively. "Well, I've got to run." Jessica kissed Cara lightly on the cheek. "Have fun tomorrow! I wish I could be there with you."

"Me, too," said Cara. She walked Jessica to the door of the apartment. "So long."

"Bye. And good luck!" Jessica whispered.

Cara wandered back to her room. She felt incredibly lonely. Lying on her bed, she touched the gold lavaliere and stared at the ceiling. "What am I going to do?" she said out loud. For the first time since Steven's proposal, Cara realized that she needed advice—and she needed it *now*. But there was no one she could turn to. All her friends would be at the party at Ken's. And would they even understand? They had all been so positive and supportive; they still thought of the elopement as an adventure, the way Cara herself had at first.

She was alone with this. Or was she? Leaving her bedroom, she prowled quietly through the apartment. She found her mother in the kitchen, doing some paperwork and drinking tea. Mrs. Walker looked surprised when Cara entered. The two of them hadn't talked a great deal since their fight the previous weekend. With so much going on, it had been easy for Cara to avoid her mother. "Hi, Mom," she said casually. "What are you working on?"

"Oh, just some office business. I have a bunch of loose ends to take care of before I leave."

Loose ends . . . Steven would have been a 'loose end,' Cara thought. Instead, she had decided to tie the loose end into a wedding knot. Suddenly, Cara wanted more than anything to share her conflict with her mother, to tell her what was in her heart. Weren't they supposed to have a mother-daughter talk the night before the wedding? But Cara just couldn't bring herself to speak.

"Cara, I've been wanting to talk to you about last weekend," Mrs. Walker said. "About the situation between me and your father."

"You don't have to explain."

"I think I do. Anyway, I want to," Mrs. Walker said. "I know it's hard for you to understand how I could appear so . . . so accepting of the fact that your father is remarrying. It *was* difficult for me to see him with Julia." Mrs. Walker's voice trembled slightly. "Very difficult."

Cara put a hand on her mother's arm. "I know, Mom."

"But I've had to come to terms with the fact that your father and I are no longer married," Mrs. Walker continued. "It took me a while, but I know now that the divorce, as hard as it's been, was best for everyone concerned. I still love you father, Cara, but things could never have worked out between us. And as strange as it might seem, because I love him I'm happy that he's found someone who's right for him."

"You are?" Cara asked softly.

"Yes, I am," Mrs. Walker said sincerely. "Love is a crazy thing. It means making sacrifices, and accepting that things can't always work out the way you want them to. I've accepted the idea of your father marrying Julia." She smiled. "I suppose I'll meet someone new myself when the time is right."

To Cara, her mother had never appeared more beautiful or more brave than she did at that moment. "I know you will, Mom."

"But in the meantime, I'm content to be single. I feel stronger and more self-confident than I've ever felt before. I'm making my own decisions, and they're good ones! That's a wonderful feeling."

"It must be," Cara said sincerely.

Mrs. Walker squeezed her daughter's arm. "I know how hard all these changes are for you. Change is like that. Exciting, but also scary. I'm scared and I know you're scared, too."

If you only knew, Cara thought a bit desperately.

Her mother got up to put the kettle on to boil for more tea. Cara fell into a reverie. Looking now at her parents' situation from the perspective her mother had given her, it began to make sense. It was better to be a strong single person than someone married for the wrong reason.

And there were good sacrifices and bad sacrifices, Cara decided. If she married Steven, she would have to give up a lot of very important things. She would be denying herself the process of discovery her mother was experiencing now, the chance to find out what kind of life she *really* wanted to live. And she would be denying Steven the same chance.

Steven was willing to sacrifice his career for Cara. Cara knew that it might be time for her to make a different kind of sacrifice for the both of them. But did she have the courage? Could she face the pain that would result from giving up her relationship with Steven in order to prevent them from ruining their lives?

Eleven

"What did your mother say when you left for a ski trip wearing a long white dress?" Steven kidded Cara on Saturday morning as they headed out of town in the VW.

"She left for the office before I even got out of bed," Cara replied. "Besides, it isn't a long dress. It's not even really white!"

She had chosen the cream-colored tea-length dress as the closest thing to a wedding dress she owned. She had worn it on a number of special occasions. She had never expected to get married in it.

Steven glanced at her out of the corner of his eye. "Well, you look beautiful. Although you look beautiful even when you're wearing jeans and a sweatshirt."

Cara smiled. "Thanks, Steven."

"I almost forgot." Keeping his eyes on the road, Steven reached around to the floor behind the driver's seat. When he brought his arm back, he was holding a bouquet wrapped in green tissue paper. "These are for you."

Cara unwrapped a big bunch of dewy pink and white roses, tied with a white satin bow. "Oh, Steven, they're gorgeous."

"You can't get married without a bouquet, even if there's no one to throw it to afterwards."

Cara breathed in the sweet scent of the roses. "I wouldn't want to throw them, anyway. I'll keep them forever."

They were on the highway now. Soon they left the green hills and valleys behind, and the horizon flattened out into a desert landscape. Steven broke the silence that had fallen over them. "Did you sleep at all last night?"

"Not a wink," Cara confessed. "That's normal, isn't it?"

Steven laughed. "I hope so, because I didn't, either. We'll probably collapse right after the ceremony. I brought a big blanket. We can find a park somewhere and have a picnic. Or we could just check into the hotel and take a nap."

Cara hesitated. "That sounds . . . nice."

Steven glanced at her. Gripping the steering wheel with his left hand, he took her hand with his right. "We're taking a pretty big step. There are going to be a lot of changes in our lives. But one thing won't change, and that's how

much I love you. So don't be nervous about . . .
tonight. All I want is to be with you. We can
take things slowly."

The tenderness in Steven's voice brought a
lump to Cara's throat. "Thanks, Steven," she
said softly. "I love you, too. So much."

"And that's what matters, right?"

She paused before responding. "Right."

The miles rolled away, and both Steven and
Cara lapsed into their own thoughts. Cara
stared out the window but she couldn't focus
on the spectacular desert scenery. Lying awake
all night, she had had plenty of time to think
about her conversation with her mother and to
consider her and Steven's predicament from
every possible angle. There was no easy solution to their problem, Cara had realized at last.
She loved Steven and he loved her, but love
wasn't an answer in itself. Love wasn't all there
was to marriage.

*If I go to London with Mom, I may never see
Steven again.* The prospect brought hot, stinging
tears to Cara's eyes. She kept her head turned
away so that Steven wouldn't see them. Breaking up now would be incredibly painful. But
Cara knew they would each get over it eventually. She also knew that if she married Steven
in order to stay in Sweet Valley, there was a
very good chance their marriage would only
end in bitterness. Steven would resent the
restrictions marriage placed on his career ambi-

tions, and Cara would resent the loss of her freedom.

Cara knew what she *should* do. It was as clear as the blue desert sky. But *how* could she do it? The wheels were in motion; the car was speeding toward Nevada. They had left Sweet Valley far behind them.

Cara had never felt so helpless. She studied Steven's calm, determined profile. He sensed her looking at him, and smiled. Cara buried her face in the roses to hide her dismay. It was too late to go back. What was she going to do?

From her bedroom window, Jessica watched her brother drive off. His skis were in the rack on top of the VW, but Jessica knew he wasn't going skiing. He was on his way to Cara's, and from there it was Nevada or bust. *I blew it*, Jessica thought morosely. Her plot to discourage Cara had failed, as had Elizabeth's final phone call to Steven the night before. There was just no stopping Steven and Cara. They were on their way. They were going through with it.

Pulling a sweatshirt on over her nightgown, Jessica padded through the bathroom that connected her room and Elizabeth's. She opened the door to Elizabeth's room quietly, but as she had expected, Elizabeth was also awake and positioned at her window.

Elizabeth turned and Jessica saw her own

dread mirrored in her twin's eyes. That clinched it. If Elizabeth was conceding defeat, then defeat it was. "It's too late," Jessica wailed, collapsing onto Elizabeth's bed in tears. "They're getting married and it's all my fault!"

"Too late," Elizabeth echoed sadly. Suddenly, her tone cleared. "No, it's not. It's not too late!"

"What do you mean?" Jessica sat up, sniffling. "They left."

"They left, but they have a long drive ahead of them," Elizabeth pointed out. "There may *still* be time to stop the wedding. *If* we do what we should have done in the first place," she added.

"Tell Mom and Dad," Jessica guessed.

"Tell Mom and Dad," Elizabeth affirmed.

"But Steven will kill us!"

"He'll want to," Elizabeth acknowledged, "and Cara won't exactly be pleased with us, either. But someday, they'll see things differently. They'll forgive us. It's the right thing to do, Jess."

Jessica knew her sister was right. She jumped up from the bed. "Come on!"

The twins dashed to their parents' bedroom; it was empty. Racing downstairs, they discovered Mr. and Mrs. Wakefield sipping coffee and reading the newspaper. Jessica stopped in the entrance, suddenly apprehensive. She glanced at Elizabeth, and saw that she was clearly thinking the same thing. Their parents weren't going to be happy about this, either!

"It sounded like a herd of elephants up there," Mr. Wakefield observed amiably. "What gets you two in motion so early on a Saturday morning?"

Jessica elbowed her sister. Elizabeth cleared her throat. "Um, we have something to tell you. It's about Steven. Steven and Cara."

"Something about the ski trip?" Mrs. Wakefield asked.

"They're not going on a ski trip," Elizabeth informed her mother. "They're driving to Nevada. To elope."

"To *elope*?" Mrs. Wakefield said in disbelief.

Elizabeth nodded. For a moment, Mr. and Mrs. Wakefield stared at their daughters. Then Mr. Wakefield jumped to his feet. "We have to go after them."

"I know where they're heading," Jessica said as her father strode toward the telephone. "I helped Steven find a chapel."

Mrs. Wakefield looked sternly at Jessica. "How long have you known about this?"

"Liz has known as long as I have!" Jessica cried in self-defense. "Well, almost as long."

"What's the Walkers' phone number?" Mr. Wakefield shouted.

Jessica told him the number. They waited in anxious silence as he dialed. "No answer," he said finally, slamming the phone down.

"Oh!" Jessica exclaimed. "I bet Mrs. Walker's at the office."

Flipping rapidly through the phone book, Mr. Wakefield located the number and dialed again. This time he reached Cara's mother. "I have some disturbing news," he announced. "According to Elizabeth and Jessica, Steven and Cara are on their way to Nevada to elope."

Jessica heard Mrs. Walker exclaim on the other end of the line. "We'll be by the office to get you in five minutes," Mr. Wakefield promised.

Hanging up the phone, he faced his daughters. His genial mood had completely vanished. Jessica hadn't seen her father this worked up in a long time. "Get some shoes on, fast," Mr. Wakefield ordered the twins. "And get in the car. They have a head start, but we might be able to catch them. You'd better *hope* we catch them," he added ominously.

Jessica gulped. She had gotten in trouble plenty of times before, but she had a feeling this could be the stunt that got her grounded for life. She whirled, jostling Elizabeth in her rush to be the first one to the stairs. "You'd better be hoping," she hissed at Elizabeth, "that Steven and Cara get a flat tire!"

"This is it!" Cara exclaimed. "Red Canyon Road. Take a left."

They were already into the intersection. The VW's tires squealed as Steven abruptly made the turn. "Sorry," Cara said meekly. "I couldn't read the sign until we were right underneath it."

Steven took a deep breath, stifling the urge to curse. It wasn't fair to let off steam at Cara's expense. It wasn't her fault they had gotten lost and had been driving in circles for fifteen minutes. Red Canyon apparently wasn't big on street signs. "It's OK," he said, managing to sound cheerful. "We're heading in the right direction now." Sure enough, a few blocks later they spotted the tiny Red Canyon town hall. Steven braked in front of it. "This is the place. The chapel's inside."

Steven got out of the car and crossed to the passenger side to open the door for Cara. She stepped out, the roses cradled in one arm.

As if by agreement, they paused for a moment on the sere, brown grass. Steven watched as she put her free hand to her hair, tucking a loose strand back into the French braid and adjusting the blue hair ribbon. With the armful of flowers and her skirt billowing in the dry desert wind, she made a beautiful picture. Steven's eyes glowed with love and pride. Cara wasn't just his girlfriend anymore; she was about to become his wife.

All at once, a strange peace, a mixture of resignation and contentment, stole over Steven's soul. He had had plenty of second thoughts. But now, as he looked into Cara's eyes and saw more love there than ever before, the last trace of doubt disappeared. *It's worth it.* Steven bent to hug Cara, gently so as to avoid crushing the flowers. "Are you ready?" he asked her.

She nodded. "Yes. I'm ready."

Steven offered his arm and together they walked into the hall.

"The justice of the peace is waiting for you," the receptionist informed them when they identified themselves. "We'll do the paperwork after the ceremony."

The chapel was at the end of the hall. Steven and Cara were silent as they approached it. *This is it,* Steven thought, straightening his shoulders.

The justice of the peace greeted them warmly, then started right in with the ceremony. *It's definitely the no-frills way to get married,* Steven thought. *It's lucky we're both sure about this!*

Steven squeezed Cara's arm. He put a hand in his blazer pocket and felt for the wedding rings as the question he had been preparing himself to answer was posed. "Steven, do you take Cara to be your lawfully wedded wife?"

Steven looked down into Cara's soft brown eyes. "I do," he answered without hesitation.

The justice of the peace then turned to Cara. "And Cara, do you take Steven to be your lawfully wedded husband?"

Cara didn't hesitate, either. "No," she said quietly.

The justice of the peace adjusted his glasses. Steven stiffened. He stared at Cara. *I can't have heard her right,* he thought.

But when Cara spoke again, her voice was clear and firm. "I'm sorry, but I can't marry you, Steven."

At that moment, the door to the chapel burst open with a bang. To Steven's further astonishment, five people dashed into the room: Cara's mother and his own parents and sisters.

"Stop the ceremony!" Mr. Wakefield commanded.

Steven looked wildly from Cara to his parents and back again. "What's going on?" he asked her, his voice cracking.

"Let me explain—" Cara touched his arm, but Steven shook off her hand. Confused and hurt, he didn't see the look of love and sorrow on her face; he didn't hear her beg him to understand and forgive her. All Steven could think was that somehow Cara and the others had planned this humiliation. But why?

"How could you do this to me?" he said hoarsely.

"Steven, I—"

He didn't wait for Cara's explanation. Hurling the wedding rings to the floor, Steven pushed his way past his family and ran out of the chapel.

Twelve

"How was your last day at Sweet Valley High?" Mrs. Walker asked Cara on Monday afternoon.

Cara dumped her book bag on the kitchen counter. "Emotional." She put a hand to her face and smiled weakly. "Just checking to see if my nose is still attached. I went through about a million tissues."

"Goodbyes are no fun," Mrs. Walker commiserated. "I said quite a few today myself."

Cara scanned the meager contents of the refrigerator. There wasn't much left in there. She closed the door and sighed. "I'm seeing all my friends again tonight at the going-away party Lila's giving me, so the hardest part today was saying goodbye to my teachers. Ms. Dalton, Mr. Collins . . . I've done my share of complaining about homework and tests over the years, but still, I'm going to miss Sweet Valley High."

"It's a special place. But your new school in London will be, too," Mrs. Walker promised.

"I'm sure it will be. Look, I still have some packing to do," Cara lied. "I'll be in my room."

"Let me know if I can help," Mrs. Walker offered.

Alone in her room, Cara sat on the edge of the bed and put her face in her hands. She was completely drained, which she supposed wasn't surprising when she considered what she had gone through in the past couple of days. She had canceled her elopement at the last possible second, and, because she hadn't gotten married, she would be leaving Sweet Valley after all. The very next day, she and her mother would be on a plane to England.

Mom's been wonderful, Cara thought. Of course, she had been upset at how close Cara had come to eloping, and disappointed that Cara had not confided in her. But Mrs. Walker was completely sympathetic to Cara's frustration in the face of circumstances over which she felt she had no control. And she also understood that leaving Steven this way was breaking Cara's heart. They had stayed up almost all Saturday night talking. Mrs. Walker had told Cara a story about her own first love, a boy who had gone to work in his father's hardware store after high school graduation. Mrs. Walker had wanted to stay with him, but her parents had insisted that she go away to college. "And that's where I met your father, and where I got the education I needed to have a career, not just a job," Mrs. Walker had concluded.

Suddenly, Cara realized that tears were streaming through her fingers. She understood the point of her mother's story, and she knew she had done the right thing at the chapel in Nevada. But Cara was certain that for as long as she lived, she would never forget Steven's face at the moment she had told him she couldn't marry him—the agony in his eyes, the betrayal. *It's not fair,* Cara thought, wiping her damp cheeks with her shirt sleeves. *Why did I have to cause so much pain to the person I love more than anyone on earth?*

When Steven had run from the chapel and sped off in his car, Cara had been terribly worried. Where was he going? What if he had an accident, driving in such a distracted state? Fortunately, Jessica had phoned her that night to tell her the Wakefields had received a terse call from Steven. Apparently he was back at the university and OK. He hadn't said much, but according to Jessica, he *had* been very clear about one thing. He didn't want to see or talk to his family, or to Cara. Especially not to Cara.

Despite the message from Jessica, Cara had tried to get in touch with Steven a number of times over the past couple of days. She had spoken to his roommate, Bob, once and he had promised to tell Steven she had called. Not surprisingly, Steven hadn't called her back.

Cara took something from her pocket: the two gold wedding bands she had picked up after Steven had tossed them away. The ring that would have been Steven's was plain but the smaller one, hers, was engraved inside. Cara read the inscription one more time, her eyes blurring with tears. *I love you. Forever, Steven.*

Quickly, she picked up the telephone and dialed Steven's dorm room. On the third ring, someone answered.

It was Steven's voice. Cara spoke fast, praying that this time he would hear her out. "Please, Steven, I have to see you before I go," she begged. "We have to talk. I still love—"

There was a click; he had hung up. Cara redialed. This time, Steven's answering machine picked up. Cara slammed down the receiver, hurt and frustrated. She didn't bother reaching for yet another tissue. There was no point in trying to stop the flow of tears. She had to face the fact that she was going to leave the country without seeing Steven again. She would never get to apologize, to explain, to hold him one last time. Their relationship—their friendship as well as their love—was over. "Forever" had come to an end.

The going-away party at Lila's had been underway for about an hour when Jessica joined Cara near the refreshment table on the patio. "Considering the fact that you're the guest of honor, you don't look like you're having a very good time," Jessica observed.

Cara ladled out a cup of punch for Jessica. "Can you blame me?"

"No," said Jessica. "If it were me, I'd still be crying."

Jessica was referring to the fact that when Cara had walked into the party at Lila's and seen the Bon Voyage and We'll Miss You banners, she had burst into tears. Cara smiled in spite of herself. "Poor Lila. My mascara ran all over her silk shirt when I hugged her."

"She'll probably never forgive you," Jessica joked.

"What about you?" Cara asked. "Have you forgiven me? Steven and I got you in some pretty deep trouble."

"Liz and I are definitely in the doghouse," Jessica admitted cheerfully. "But we're not really in trouble. When the heat of the moment wore off, Mom and Dad decided they couldn't hold us responsible. I guess they decided all's well that ends well."

Cara sighed. *All's well that ends well.* That wasn't the way it felt from her perspective.

Carrying their cups of punch, Jessica and Cara sat down on two folding chairs set up next to the pool. It was a good spot for people-watching. The music was great and there was a crowd dancing on the other side of the pool.

Cara was glad to see her friends were having fun, even if she wasn't. "Who's that talking to Todd?" she asked.

Jessica looked over to where Todd and a girl were engaged in an animated conversation. "Oh, some sophomore," Jessica said dismissively. "She's been following him around all night like a puppy dog. Pretty pathetic."

"She's cute," Cara observed.

"Yeah, I suppose," Jessica agreed without much interest. "But Todd doesn't go for cute." She smiled slyly. "He goes for drop-dead gorgeous."

Cara laughed. "Of course. How could I forget? That's why he's dating your identical twin sister."

Jessica took another look at Todd and the girl and frowned. "Come to think of it, I hope *Todd* hasn't forgotten."

"I'm sure he hasn't. So, I guess Elizabeth's not coming," Cara said somewhat sadly.

"Don't take it personally. It's just that she's hurt because Steven's hurt. I mean, she's not mad at you or anything. She asked me to say goodbye to you for her. She just didn't want to see you right now, that's all."

"She doesn't have to worry." Cara bit her lip, determined not to start crying again. "She'll never see me again, and neither will Steven."

"Well, if it's any consolation, I don't think I'm ever going to see him again, either," Jessica told Cara. "For some reason he's furious at me, maybe because I'm the one who talked him into deciding to get married in the first place."

"Talked him into it?"

Jessica told Cara about *Love Story* and the sudden inspiration she had shared with Steven. "Believe me, though, sooner or later he would have thought of it on his own."

"He *was* pretty impulsive," Cara admitted, recalling the rainy afternoon when Steven had rushed over to her apartment to propose to her. "But then, so was I." It was truly ironic, Cara thought. If she had said "no" that day, Steven would be here with her now. "Jessica, I *can't* go away without explaining why I wouldn't marry Steven," Cara announced.

"But he doesn't want to talk to you," Jessica pointed out. "He won't even answer your phone calls!"

"I know. I can't tell him directly. But maybe I can find another way to reach him." Cara hopped to her feet. "I'm going to call Elizabeth!"

"Elizabeth? What's the point of calling her?"

Cara was already hurrying toward the house. "I'll explain later!"

Cara found a telephone in the Fowler Crest library. She hesitated before dialing the Wakefields' phone number. Should she just drive over to their house while she had her nerve up? No, she couldn't face Mr. and Mrs. Wakefield. Tears jumped to Cara's eyes as she remembered how well she had always gotten along with Steven's parents. But she *had* to see

Elizabeth. Cara knew Steven talked about serious things, personal things, more often with Elizabeth than he did with Jessica. If Cara couldn't explain to Steven directly, she could at least explain to Elizabeth, and maybe someday Elizabeth would speak to her brother on Cara's behalf.

Elizabeth answered the phone. "Liz, it's Cara." Cara knew she sounded nervous, and her nervousness grew when she heard the distance in Elizabeth's usually warm voice.

"Uh, hi, Cara."

"Elizabeth, I know it's probably the last thing you want to do, but I wonder if you would meet me at the Dairi Burger. Just for a few minutes. I need to talk to you."

"I'm kind of busy. I have a newspaper story due tomorrow."

"Please." Cara's voice trembled. "It's important."

"Well . . . OK," Elizabeth agreed reluctantly. "I'll be at the Dairi Burger in fifteen minutes."

When Cara got to the Dairi Burger, she sat down at a corner booth to wait for Elizabeth. When she entered the restaurant, Cara waved.

Elizabeth stopped on her way to Cara's booth to exchange a few words with a group of boys from school. Cara saw that one of them couldn't take his eyes off Elizabeth; turning in his chair, he stared after her as she continued on to join Cara. "Don't look now, but you have an admirer," Cara told her.

Elizabeth smiled. "I've noticed. We don't know each other very well, but lately it seems like everywhere I go, he pops up to say hi to me."

"He's pretty cute. It must be flattering," Cara commented.

Elizabeth fidgeted with a menu, not meeting Cara's eyes. "Yeah, I guess it is."

After a long pause, Cara said simply, "I'm sorry."

Elizabeth shrugged. "What happened was between you and Steven."

"Anything that touches Steven touches his family, too," Cara continued. "Would you be any happier if I'd gone through with the ceremony?"

Elizabeth laughed. "No, I don't suppose I would be!"

Cara's face grew serious again. "Liz, I know you think I'm completely heartless. But I had a good reason for doing what I did. I love Steven with all my heart."

Elizabeth looked doubtful. "If you love him, how could you have hurt him like that?"

"It's *because* I love him that I had to break things off. When we decided to elope, we hadn't taken the time to think about all the changes marriage would bring. I finally understood that marriage wasn't the answer. I really wanted to stay with Steven. But if we'd gotten married, I would have prevented him from becoming the person he wanted to be—the person *I* wanted him to be, the person I wanted to be with. I finally realized that no matter how much I wanted us to stay together, it wouldn't have been right to preserve our relationship at the expense of our individual lives. The night before we were supposed to elope, Jessica told me about the letter from the law program. I *couldn't* let Steven give that up for me." Cara's eyes misted. "Can you understand, Elizabeth? If it were you and Todd, wouldn't you have done the same thing?"

Her own eyes damp, Elizabeth nodded.

"Well, I feel a little better." Cara dabbed her eyes with a paper napkin. "He won't see me. He won't even talk to me on the phone. But explaining things to you is the next best thing to talking to him."

Elizabeth nodded again. "Next time I see him, I'll tell him that you and I talked," she promised. "I think it will make him feel better to hear this."

In the parking lot, Cara and Elizabeth hugged. "Good luck, Cara," Elizabeth said. "Have a safe trip to England. What a wonderful adventure!"

For the first time, Cara felt a twinge of excitement at the prospect of the new life ahead of her. "I'll miss you, Liz."

"I'll miss you, too." Elizabeth looked solemnly at Cara. "And so will Steven. I'll be sure to talk to him, when the time is right."

"Thanks. I guess I should go back to the party at Lila's. Want to come?"

143

"No." Elizabeth smiled. "I really do have an article to write!"

Cara waved as Elizabeth drove off in the Fiat. Her spirits felt lighter than they had in weeks. It helped to have straightened things out with Elizabeth. Cara simply had to believe that someday, somehow, Steven would forgive her. *And who knows?* she thought, walking slowly to her own car. Maybe someday, somewhere, she and Steven would meet again.

Thirteen

Tuesday morning, Elizabeth lay in bed watching the pale pink light of dawn fill her room. She had tossed and turned all night, haunted by her memory of Cara's sadness at the Dairi Burger and by the thought of her leaving Sweet Valley forever while Steven hid himself away at college, nursing his wounds. Steven and Cara's relationship had to end one way or another, but Elizabeth knew that the pain for the both of them was a thousand times worse because it was ending in misunderstanding.

Suddenly, Elizabeth knew what she had to do. Cara had asked Elizabeth to explain to Steven someday why she had refused to marry him. *Why should I wait for 'someday'?* Elizabeth leapt out of bed. With Cara flying to New York that day and then on to London, there was no time to waste!

Her eye on the clock, Elizabeth threw on khaki pants and a blue polo shirt. It was pretty early, but she would still be late for school by the time she drove back down from the university. But that was OK; Steven's peace of mind was worth a late slip.

Minutes later, shifting the Fiat into fifth gear, Elizabeth sped north on the coast highway. It was a crystal-clear morning. Everything sparkled—the vivid green palms and pines, the silvery dune grass, the wave-dashed Pacific Ocean. It was as if southern California was at its most beautiful to say goodbye to Cara, Elizabeth thought fancifully.

The university campus was quiet. Only a handful of early risers with backpacks over their shoulders wandered across the quad in the direction of the dining hall. As Elizabeth entered Steven's dorm, it occurred to her that Steven might not even be awake yet. She prepared herself for a lukewarm reception at best; she could only hope his mood would change for the better when he learned why she had come.

Elizabeth tapped lightly on the outer door of Steven and Bob's suite. To her surprise, someone answered right away, "Come in."

She pushed the door open. Steven was sitting on the sofa, wearing sweatpants and a rumpled T-shirt and holding a steaming cup of coffee. "Liz! What are you doing here?"

146

Relieved that her brother wasn't annoyed by her unexpected visit, Elizabeth sat down next to him. She quickly took in his weary, dejected appearance. "I know it's early, but I have something to tell you and it just couldn't wait," she began. "Actually, Cara has something to tell you."

Steven lifted the coffee cup, narrowing his eyes against the steam. "She said everything there was to say when she said no," he said gruffly.

"No, she didn't." Quickly, Elizabeth recounted her conversation with Cara. "Jessica read the letter from the law program and on Friday she told Cara about it," Elizabeth said in conclusion. "Apparently, finding out that you were planning to give up the law program for her was what finally convinced her that the two of you needed to be free to live your own lives."

"But why didn't she tell me sooner?" Steven wondered. "Why did she wait until we were standing in front of the justice of the peace?"

"I guess until the very last minute she couldn't quite bring herself to give up her hope that you might somehow stay together," Elizabeth surmised. "She still loves you. She didn't want to let you go."

His sister's words brought a transformation to Steven's face. His sad, bitter expression faded and his eyes brightened with joy. Just as quickly, however, they darkened again with despair. "It's too late," he moaned. "She's gone."

Elizabeth looked at her watch. "I'm pretty sure her flight to New York doesn't leave for another hour and a half."

Steven's voice was husky with hope and longing. "If I could see her one more time, just to say goodbye . . ."

"There's still time for you to get to the airport!"

Steven didn't hesitate. In less than a minute, he had combed his hair, stuck his feet into sneakers and his arms into the sleeves of a denim jacket, and grabbed his car keys. He and Elizabeth raced out the door together. "Good luck!" she called as he jumped in the VW and revved the engine. Steven waved. A moment later, his car was out of sight. Elizabeth sighed. Feeling as if some of Steven's weariness had transferred itself to her, she settled herself behind the wheel of the Fiat and drove slowly back to Sweet Valley.

Steven hit morning rush hour traffic on his way to the airport. Shifting gears rapidly, accelerating and braking, then accelerating again, he dodged in and out among the crawling cars. A few irate drivers honked, but Steven didn't care. He was determined. Nothing was going to prevent him from reaching the airport in time to say goodbye to Cara.

Deep in his heart, Steven had never stopped believing in Cara and her love for him. But his pride had been badly bruised. Elizabeth's story had freed him from the unhappiness that had been weighing him down since Saturday. *And since before Saturday*, Steven recognized as he parked the car in the airport lot. He had struggled with the same misgivings as had Cara. In the end, it was Cara who had had more insight and courage.

The drive from campus had taken an hour; there was no time to lose. Inside the airport, Steven raced to the nearest arrivals/departures display monitor. There was only one flight to New York in the next half hour. That had to be it. And it was boarding now!

Steven sprinted in the direction of gate A-5, weaving in and out among the pedestrians in much the same way that he had woven through the traffic on the highway. As he neared the gate, he heard the fatal announcement. "Flight eight-twenty to New York City is now boarding. All passengers please report to gate A-5."

Steven hurdled over a pile of luggage and then came to a stop. As his eyes swept the crowd gathered near the gate, desperately searching for Cara and her mother, panic seized him. *They're already on board*, he thought, turning away dejectedly. *I'm too late*. Then Steven spotted a girl with glossy brown hair falling in a shining cascade as she bent to pick up a small carry-on suitcase. It was Cara!

If Steven had any lingering doubts about Cara's love for him, they were dispelled now. The look of joy on her face when she saw him striding toward her was all the proof he would ever need. Cara dropped the suitcase; Steven swept her up in his arms, clasping her as tightly as he could. "Oh, Steven!" Cara was laughing and crying at the same time. "I thought I was never going to see you again. I know I disappointed you but I did it because—"

Setting her back on her feet, Steven silenced her with a gentle kiss. "I know why," he told her. "Cara, we have so little time. We shouldn't waste it on explanations. I understand and I love you."

"Oh, Steven, I love you, too." Tears sparkled in Cara's eyes. "I can't tell you what it means to me that I've had the chance to tell you that, to see you one more time."

"Let me just look at you." For a moment, Steven and Cara just stood with their arms around each other, staring into each other's eyes. Steven could see all the happiness he had ever shared with Cara reflected in her beautiful brown eyes. "I'll miss you," he said, his voice deep with emotion. "But, Cara, no matter how much time and distance come between us, I'll always love you."

"And I'll always love you, Steven." Cara pressed something into his hand. Steven felt the coolness of gold: the wedding rings. "Forever," she whispered.

After promising to write each other, there was time for one last bittersweet kiss and then Cara joined her mother. Steven watched them step through the gate to the waiting plane. Cara was gone.

He remained standing there for a few minutes longer, oblivious to the bustle of the crowd around him. A sadness settled over Steven's heart but it wasn't the heavy, oppressive sadness he had felt only that morning. With it came peace and acceptance. He would miss Cara terribly; he would miss her for a long time to come. But Steven knew he would never forget her or the love they had shared. Putting a hand in his jacket pocket, he felt an envelope. The acceptance letter from the law program. It wasn't too late to tell them that he wanted to enroll. Steven smiled. This goodbye was very different from the one he had said to Tricia. Then, there had been no future. Now, Steven knew that both he and Cara had wonderful futures ahead of them, even though they wouldn't be spending them together after all.

"Goodbye, Cara," he whispered. Turning away from the gate, Steven walked back the way he had come.

"It's just not the same without Cara," Jessica observed on Saturday. She rolled over on her beach towel with a sigh.

Lila squeezed some suntan lotion onto one of her slim, bronzed legs. "Feel sorry for yourself if you want, but I wouldn't bother feeling sorry for Cara," she advised. "She's in London right now, probably having the time of her life."

Elizabeth and Enid had spread out their towels a few feet from Jessica, Lila, and Amy. Now, Elizabeth pulled a book and a pair of sunglasses out of her tote bag, and wondered if Lila was right. *Was* Cara having the time of her life? Did she have any regrets about not marrying Steven and staying in Sweet Valley?

"We gave her a great going-away party, anyway," recalled Amy.

"*I* gave her a great going-away party," Lila corrected her. "Too bad you missed it, Liz."

"I had a lot of work to do that night," Elizabeth explained. "I said goodbye to Cara on my own."

"I must say it was surprising, seeing Todd out by himself without his better half," Lila remarked.

Elizabeth tensed slightly, sensitive to the prying note in Lila's voice. Still, she supposed it was natural for people to notice that Todd had shown up at the party without her. There was a reason why Jessica gave Elizabeth a hard time about she and Todd being inseparable. When it came to parties, the two of them always went together. If one of them couldn't or didn't want to go, the other would skip the party, too. Elizabeth herself had been surprised when Todd

152

decided to attend the weeknight going-away party without her.

"I guess he just wanted to help send Cara off in style," Elizabeth said lightly.

"He helped send her off in style, all right," Amy commented. "Talk about dancing up a storm!"

Dancing up a storm? Elizabeth thought. When she had asked Todd about the party afterward, he had said it was just OK.

"It wasn't Todd's fault," Jessica hurried to inform her sister. "That girl just wouldn't leave him alone."

"What girl?" Elizabeth asked.

Jessica pointed down the beach. "*That* girl."

Elizabeth put a hand to her forehead to shield her eyes from the bright afternoon sun. On the hard sand near the shore, Winston, Todd, and a pretty, dark-haired girl in a skimpy black bikini were setting up a volleyball net. As Elizabeth watched, the girl picked up a volleyball. She tried a serve, and laughed when the ball bounced short of the net. Laughing, too, Todd stepped up behind her. Taking her hands in his, he guided her arms to demonstrate a proper serve.

Elizabeth knew the other girls were witnessing this scene as well. "I wouldn't worry, Liz," Amy was quick to say. "I'm pretty sure Peggy knows Todd's taken."

Elizabeth frowned. From what she could see, the question was not what *Peggy* thought, but what *Todd* thought. He certainly wasn't acting as if he were "taken." A queasy, anxious feeling in her stomach, Elizabeth thought back to the conversations she and Todd had had about Steven and Cara's relationship. She remembered Todd's intense reaction that night at the Dairi Burger when he had first learned the news. In Todd's opinion, Steven and Cara were too young to know what they wanted. They were making a mistake by tying themselves down, denying themselves the opportunity to try new things and meet new people.

Suddenly, a painful suspicion crept into Elizabeth's heart. *Maybe Todd wasn't just talking about Cara and Steven. Maybe he was talking about us. Maybe* he's *the one feeling tied down.*

Todd had made it clear that he thought getting married at so young an age was a mistake. Elizabeth watched as Todd and Peggy sprinted to the ocean's edge, still laughing. Elizabeth wondered. Was Todd starting to think going steady was a mistake, too?

Is this the end for Elizabeth and Todd? Find out in Sweet Valley High #84, **THE STOLEN DIARY.**